(Book 9 of the FTL Series)
by Michael McCloskey
Copyright 2017 Michael McCloskey
ISBN: 978-1545165584

Learn more about Michael McCloskey's works at
www.squidlord.com

Cover art by Stephan Martiniere
Edited by Stephen 'Shoe' Shoemaker

Special thanks to
Maarten Hofman and Wesley Twombly

Chapter 1

The interior of the new *Iridar*—Telisa had lost track of how many of them there had been so far—gleamed. Of course, it felt different than the Vovokan ship they had lost. Most of all, it *smelled* different, she decided. The UNSF ship had been designed as a commando insertion and extraction vessel: it was small and maneuverable, yet with relatively high crew capacity.

Telisa sat beside Magnus in the mess hall. Caden, Siobhan, and Marcant sat across from them while Lee and Cynan hovered nearby.

"Good to be back in a real Terran ship, right?" Caden said cheerfully.

"Eh, it's kind of clunky," Magnus said.

"The gravity spinner is better than any Terran one I've seen," Siobhan commented.

"Yes. Shiny's been helping out the Space Force in a lot of areas. This spinner is strong and precise," Telisa said.

The *Iridar* had just set out for the Celaran homeworld. The experienced PIT team members knew the drill—it was time to talk about how to allocate their time during the trip. Even though the voyages afforded some rest and relaxation, it was also the best time to perform their rigorous VR training.

Telisa started with the obvious.

"Cynan has decided to come with us. He'll be valuable in making some kind of connection with any group of cyborg Celarans we might find."

"Is that likely?" Caden asked.

"Optimistically, yes," Telisa said. "If we find more Destroyers instead, then we'll run away and search elsewhere. Lee and Cynan have a list of star systems that other Celarans may have fled to."

Everyone seemed to like that idea, so Telisa moved on.

"I'm happy to announce that Lee has been officially accepted into the PIT team."

I said officially and PIT in the same sentence. Ha.

The Terrans clapped while Lee flitted about energetically and flickered her chevrons.

"Thank you!" she said on the channel.

Telisa let Lee enjoy that for a moment, then moved to the next item on her agenda.

"I said we would rely more on stealth this time out, and I meant it. We need to change our equipment to reflect that. We have our Celaran cloaking spheres now, and they can absorb a lot of sound, but projectile weapons are too noisy."

Telisa stood and walked around the table as she continued. "I think our main weapons should be lasers. If you want to keep a backup projectile weapon, that's fine... we never know when those might prove more effective. I'm carrying an edged weapon, laser pistol, breaker claw, and cloaking sphere. I suggest you do the same."

Everyone mulled that over.

"Any other ideas for equipment changes based on the new approach?" Telisa asked.

"We should all be in stealth suits for redundancy," suggested Siobhan. "They could hide us if the spheres get damaged or run low on power."

"Hold on there," Magnus said. "I'm giving up my rifle already. Now you want me to give up my Momma Veer?"

Telisa laughed out loud.

By the Five, that felt good.

"Sounds like a good idea, but I'll leave it voluntary," Telisa said.

Lee seemed to finally calm down from the announcement about her and grabbed a rod to hang from. Just for fun, Telisa hopped up and grabbed an adjacent hang line, then whipped her feet up and over it so she could hang from behind her knees. She dangled upside down next to Lee.

"I've never seen you do that!" exclaimed Lee.

"There are tree climbers among our ancestors," Telisa told her playfully. "We weren't always tromping around in the mud."

Lee glowed again, but no speech came through on the channel.

She must have found that funny. Or did she send a private comment to Cynan?

The Celaran cyborg floated idly the whole time. Cynan had no nervous energy to burn like the other Celarans Telisa had observed. She wondered if the cyborgs were usually very old when they decided to get augmented bodies.

"We have a good supply of attendants," Telisa said. "Remember, though, it can be tricky to divide them between intra- and extra-cloaking envelope duties. Moving them in and out of the envelope can give you away."

"Three attendants works well in the simulations," said Caden. "One to move ahead and scout around, two to stay cloaked with you."

Telisa nodded. It felt strange to nod while upside down. The blood was not rushing to her head; yet another superiority of a Trilisk host body.

"Are Adair and Achaius in the battle spheres?" asked Caden.

Marcant cleared his throat.

"They're in control of the battle spheres, but Adair and Achaius have merged their cores with attendants," Marcant said. "In fact, these two right here," he said, indicating the spheres that hovered on-station near his head.

"Come up with a few configurations, and we'll test and practice in VR," Telisa said. "Cynan is going to

3

construct two types of environments we can add to our training regimen: one for the projected condition of Celara, and another that contains a Celaran space station."

"What are they like, roughly speaking?" asked Caden.

"Cynan will send you a peek when they're ready. I imagine the space station would be very similar to the one that had been taken over by Blackvines: dwellings floating in wide open spaces."

"Correct. The homeworld should have similarities to the healthy planet we left," Cynan said. "It has support spikes and vines, though the vines were reddish and sickly when we abandoned it. The vegetative mass is greatly reduced overall. Some areas may be devoid of vines altogether."

Lee flashed in distress. Her serpentine body drooped, losing its curl.

Many of her physical cues to mood are easy to identify, Telisa thought.

"Okay, two shifts of three are your own," she announced. "The third shift is for training. I'll identify which ones everybody should be involved in. Otherwise, go ahead and group up however it shakes out each day, but be sure to mix it up sometimes. Improve your worst matchups."

Telisa looked at Marcant and thought that Adair and Achaius should probably rotate in with everyone else. She made a note to mention it to him privately.

That makes nine of us. Can I get everyone through this expedition alive?

"Okay, that's it for now. Magnus and I would like to stay and speak privately with Cynan and Lee," she said.

Too mysterious.

"I'm going to sync with them about the Shiny situation," she clarified.

Caden and Siobhan stood together and nodded to Telisa, then walked out. Marcant moved more slowly, but he did not linger. Telisa waited until they had all left.

"Shiny is the first living alien Terrans ever encountered," Telisa started. "We worked together with him to escape a Trilisk complex that had trapped us. We soon learned that his behavior was more dangerous than we had anticipated."

Lee dropped from the perch and started to glide around the room. "Dangerous? He protects your home planet, doesn't he?"

"We think it's only because it's best for him. He has on several occasions taken over everything whether we were comfortable with it or not. The Vovokans were a loose collection of warlords before the Quarus war, and to him, cooperation is known, but never sticky. He can quickly switch to 'competition mode' and that means he might do anything—even kill us—if that became his best move."

"Our planets could be in danger," Cynan concluded. "Shiny could hurt Earth, or he could hurt our colony planet."

"The strange thing is, Earth doesn't care. He's taken over there, and everyone's happier than ever before. We don't know if it's because he really is doing a great job, or if there's also some subtle way that he's using the Trilisk technology to influence public opinion."

"We hang from the same branch now, but I feel an urge to warn other Celarans of the danger," Cynan said.

"Yes. I knew that telling you would mean telling other Celarans," Telisa said. "I felt you had to know the truth, and yet, at the same time, these are only our fears, the PIT team's fears. You should come to your own conclusions. I beg you to be cautious, that's all. Lean on Shiny, for now, to rebuild your civilization. Just know that the day may come when you can't lean on him anymore."

Michael McCloskey

Chapter 2

Celara Palnod was a planet ten percent less massive than Earth. Marcant did not need the many advanced sensors of the *Iridar* to tell him this planet had seen a catastrophe. A quick glance at the magnified video feed told him that. Roiling clouds of gray ash obscured a fourth of its surface. The rest was a combination of ocean blue and mottled red-brown land masses.

Marcant pored over the readings coming in. Telisa had asked him to summarize the planetary scans for the team, a responsibility that had likely come to him because of the loss of Cilreth.

No doubt everyone already knew they had arrived and would be preparing themselves for action.

What will they want to know first?

"The Celaran population," suggested Adair. "I'll devise a counting method."

"Thank you," Marcant said. "I think we also need an analysis of—"

"The vine cover, yes," Achaius said. "I suppose you want me to do that."

Marcant smiled. That was Achaius's way of offering help while pretending to be above it all.

"Most helpful, Achaius," Marcant said. "I'll turn my attention outward, then," he said.

Telisa made a private connection to Marcant.

"Marcant, since you're gathering data on the planet, I'll concentrate on spotting any alien ships or stations in the system," Telisa said.

"Good. Thank you," Marcant said. "We should have a preliminary report in ten or twenty more minutes."

What does that leave me? Hrm. How about Celaran buildings and infrastructure?

Marcant focused on artificial constructs detected on the planet. They had lost a lot of data when the last *Iridar* crashed and burned, but the new ship had been at the colony and it knew how to spot Celaran buildings. Marcant used those signatures to find the same kinds of structures below. The countless damaged buildings registered as partial matches; Marcant trained the processes that analyzed the scanner data to recognize buildings that had been heavily damaged, then continued until it could see even the smoldering foundations.

The analyzer then grouped every Celaran structure it saw into various states of damage. Marcant watched the information aggregate. The vast majority of the Celaran signature hits piled up in the categories for destroyed structures.

The planet has been crushed. Less than one percent of the buildings are left intact.

Marcant checked on his friends' findings.

The vine data was still being collected, but so far, it was staying below one percent of the norm for the other Celaran planets they had visited.

Marcant looked at a distribution of the healthy vines and investigated the peak points. The planetary map spun in his PV, highlighting each in turn. He saw small areas on islands and plateaus where the vines were healthy.

These will be good places to visit.

He then turned his attention to Adair's population counting. Instead of one count, he found many and realized in another few seconds that Adair was counting many different life forms. Adair must have sensed his reads of the data.

"There are some oddities here," Adair said. "I think the feral flyers, the smaller ones, mostly died out. That makes sense given the global loss of vegetation. But I do see a larger form of fauna, very similar to Celarans."

Marcant viewed several images of the creatures taken from above. They were larger than any Celaran he had seen, an average of a meter longer with a much wider shape.

Marcant decided to seek out help before sending out the initial report.

"Lee, Cynan, are these native animals?"

He sent pointers out to the Celarans. As he expected, Cynan reacted quickly.

"Those are unfamiliar. They are... very similar to us."

"They're flying higher than I would normally," Lee added. "These data suggest not only a different appearance but very different behavior."

Marcant saw that there were millions of the creatures gliding high above the planet's surface.

"Telisa will want to investigate. Tag the map with any large concentrations of these," Marcant said to Adair.

"There are no large concentrations, but they do tend to glide in flocks," Adair said. "I'll make note of the most accessible groups."

"Here, can you choose some close to these areas with surviving vines? We can reduce the amount of travel we'll have to do."

"Sure."

"Thank you."

"Marcant, what do you have for us?" Telisa sent from elsewhere on the ship.

"Do you want to help me report the findings?" Marcant asked Adair and Achaius.

"No way," Achaius said. "That's what we keep you around for."

"Yes, our jelly-brain ambassador," Adair said.

Marcant nodded, even though no one was looking. He gathered his thoughts and brought up a summary pane in his personal view. Then he opened a connection to the team channel.

"There are Celarans down there," Marcant announced. "The numbers are small... maybe twenty million of them."

"That must be a pitiful number," Adair said privately to Marcant and Achaius. "Surely there were millions more before the attack."

Marcant continued with the delivery of grim news.

"The vine mass is less than one percent of the colony planet we left. As expected, it's mostly unhealthy."

"Mostly?" Telisa prompted.

"I see a handful of... oases. Mostly on islands and other geographically isolated spots." He cross-indexed the locations with the Celaran populations and found a correlation. "There are concentrations of Celarans there, where the food is."

"Survivors," Caden said.

"I wonder if the Quarus will come back to annihilate the rest," Siobhan said.

"As you would expect from all this, the industrial and technological state of the planet is grave. I believe the Destroyers must have struck at all the major population centers early on. What buildings remain are scattered."

No one commented, so Marcant continued. "I read small amounts of radio usage, widely scattered. No active gravity spinners detected, though we do know that the Celarans are capable of hiding that. It may be that there are other Celaran hideouts that still have advanced technology operating."

He pointed the team at the information Adair had collected about the wide Celaran-like creatures.

"Here is an oddity that feels important. Lee and Cynan say these creatures are not native to Celara Palnod, though they clearly look similar to Celarans. There are millions of them on the planet."

"Could they be the result of a mutagenic poison?" Siobhan asked suddenly.

Marcant smiled. He did not think so—but decided to let Cynan answer.

"Highly unlikely," Cynan said. "My only theory is that they're Celarans who've been intentionally modified to survive the new environment."

That makes sense, but didn't they have other recourses?

"Would Terrans morph themselves before they would simply move to a different planet?" asked Caden, clearly thinking along the same lines as Marcant.

"And aren't Celarans even more likely to run than Terrans?" asked Siobhan.

"Celarans are not all like me and those on my vine," Lee said. "It's also possible that there are no means of escape left. Modifying bodies would have been easy, as long as facilities remained to do so. The refugees may have had no other vine to choose."

"Continue to gather information," Telisa said. "Come up with a list of sites to investigate."

"To make contact?" Marcant asked.

"Not immediately. We only want to observe for now," Telisa said. "Siobhan and Caden. You're up first."

Marcant was not surprised. Those two would see taking point as an exciting opportunity. He was glad he would not be going first.

"Maybe I'm finally getting through to you, jelly-brain," Adair said to Marcant approvingly.

"Is there any good news?" Telisa asked with a sigh.

"No Trilisk activity detected," Marcant said.

"Good. I saw no signs of spacecraft or space stations, Celaran, Quarus, or otherwise," Telisa said.

"If there are spacecraft, they would be cloaked," Cynan pointed out.

"Would we see them?" Telisa asked.

"Hrm. Probably not. Not with this ship," Marcant said. "We should have taken a Celaran ship. Or at least, brought one."

"Yes I agree, this is suboptimal," Achaius said.

"The Celarans might well have refused to send one anyway," Adair said. "They needed every last ship just to survive."

"The Space Force is there now," Achaius pointed out.

"Would you trust the alien fleet to protect you when your whole civilization is at risk?"

"I would not."

"Then why are we arguing?" Adair asked.

"Yes, why?" Marcant inquired of both of them.

They took the hint and shut up.

"Keep working the data," Telisa said. "Also, use four or more of the ship's probes to keep patrolling the rest of the system for a Celaran or Destroyer presence. The handful of attendants I have out there aren't really enough. I want more details before we choose our destinations."

"Launching the probes..."

Marcant gave the probes a complex spiral course through the system, looping around the other four planets to save energy and discover anything hiding away. Then he went back to the sensor feeds of the planet below.

This is going to be a grim mission.

Chapter 3

The nearby ruins dominated the horizon before Caden. They could be seen from within the sickly red jungle because the vines climbed to less than half the height of the support spikes. Most of the biomass here had dried and fallen, congealing into a flaky brown mush. Small red insects that reminded him of maggots writhed in colonies every few meters.

Siobhan and Lee were nothing but two abstract avatars moving along beside him. Siobhan's echoform image was a ghostly blue humanoid while Lee's writhed like a snake swimming through the air. With the three-man squad using the cloaking devices, the echoforms were all they could see of each other. Caden was used to it by now since they had been training this way on the *Iridar* for a week.

Caden watched Lee's echoform glide along the broken ground. The Celaran had talked Telisa into letting her join the initial recon team. Lee moved slowly, which Caden had learned was a sign of sadness.

"Many of these spikes are dead," Lee said. Caden recalled that here on their planet of origin, the soaring support spikes were natural growths, unlike their artificial equivalents on the colony worlds.

That explains why some of these spikes are pale like bone and others have the greenish tint. I assume the greenish ones are still alive.

"These red bugs are native, right?" Siobhan asked.

"Yes," Lee said. "They are scavengers. Ground things."

The translator indicated her last statement was in light disgust.

Ground things. Ha.

"Lee, take a quick fly-through and let me know if you see any of the survivors," Telisa ordered from the *Iridar*. "Make no contact. Stay hidden."

The team's three extra-envelope attendants routed Telisa's communications to them. Lee and Cynan had shown the Terrans all the ins and outs of staying in touch even while the cloaking spheres were active. They had been taught that, though communication was possible, and still quite stealthy by Terran standards, it might give them away to advanced observers.

Caden and Siobhan picked their way toward the dull gray and green hulks of dead buildings in the distance. The orbital survey had told them about a hundred Celarans lived in this area. Caden hooked into a feed from a scout attendant. No life other than the bugs was visible from its vantage point. He could not make out any signs of recent repairs in the ruins.

The buildings were made in the same crazy style of the ones Caden had seen on the colony worlds and the space habitat. Few of their circular windows had survived the destruction. Unlike heavily damaged Terran buildings that revealed the crisscross pattern of sundered floors and rooms, the Celaran building shells exposed hollow interiors lined with small niches along the walls and floor serving as individual 'rooms'. For the first time, Caden understood why the Celaran buildings were so chaotic: the highly varied outer surface features gave the internal niches different shapes and sizes to match them to various usages.

Caden looked back the way they had come and saw the line of their footsteps imprinted in the brown mush, visible just outside their cloaking envelopes.

"We're leaving a trail," Caden pointed out. "Let's try to stay close to the lowest vines to cover it."

"Good idea," Siobhan said. "Oh, look."

Caden figured she referred to Lee's video feed. Lee had come across a wide swath of devastation that cut through the cluster of destroyed buildings. He recognized the cause immediately.

The main weapons of a Colossal ripped right through the center.

Caden and Siobhan stood a half kilometer from the nearest building. It was an outlier; it looked about two Terran stories tall. Its complex roof was brown, indicating it had been under the vine canopy before the disaster and now sat covered in the mush.

I wish I had my sniper rifle, Caden thought. *Its powerful long-range sensors might be useful in spotting something.*

He settled for sending his third attendant to circle the building ahead.

"There's one!" Siobhan said.

Caden quickly located the feed she spoke of before she sent out a pointer. A Celaran flashed brightly inside the wreck of a building missing an entire side. Siobhan's scout attendant had spotted it.

The Celaran's signal quickly brought two other Celarans to it. They hovered over a ruined machine.

"What are they doing?" Caden wondered.

"Scavenging power stores," Lee answered quickly. "They've probably come here to find useful items to bring back to wherever they live now."

Caden saw from the tactical and video feeds that Lee had circled back toward the Celarans they had spotted. He stopped with Siobhan over 100 meters away from the Celarans. They could watch the aliens through the video feeds of the forward attendants, so there was no reason to get any closer.

One of the Celarans dropped onto the machine and held onto it with the fingers on one end of its body, while it used a tool rod held in its other fingers to detach an outer plate. Then another Celaran dropped down and helped the first pry pieces out of the machine.

They probably have no factories working around here, Caden thought. *Now they're reduced to looting the ruins and taking anything useful.*

"Magnus says get samples, please," Telisa said. She had been the only one talking to the ground team because she wanted to minimize radio traffic to avoid detection.

"Should we use an attendant?" Caden asked.

"No. Magnus whipped up a couple of collection bots," Siobhan said. "It was a last-minute thing."

Caden could not see Siobhan, but he assumed she was retrieving machines from her pack. He supposed the things must be small so to avoid alarming a Celaran.

But won't they find those bots' behavior unusual?

He decided to hold the criticism until he saw the bots.

"There," Siobhan said. "There they go."

"Where?"

"Those bugs," Siobhan said.

Caden looked around. He saw two insects flying away through the vines toward the Celarans they had seen.

"Ah, disguised well. Native bugs too, I presume?"

"Yes, I think Lee helped with them."

"Why don't we simply ask them for samples? We could trade some of our equipment for it," Caden suggested.

"No direct contact yet," Telisa repeated.

"Shouldn't we render aid?" asked Siobhan.

"We're going to help them. All of them. By keeping the team safe and making contact with factions we can ally with to defeat the Destroyers. Handing out what few trinkets we have to random survivors won't change the big picture."

"Wow. Telisa sounds... harder now," Siobhan said to Caden privately.

"Still, the plan sounds noble enough," Caden said to her. "What are the samples for?" he asked Telisa.

"Lee said we could tell a lot about their health by analyzing tiny flakes of their skin."

Their robotic collectors flew up the Celarans as they worked. The aliens did not notice anything amiss as the duo of artificial insects buzzed straight toward the group. The bots simultaneously collided with their targets, bouncing right off the aliens' exposed integument. The two Celarans that had been struck abandoned their work and flitted about the room in obvious distress.

"I hope they're just scared," Caden said.

"They're startled," Lee said. "Not hurt. The tiny machines are flying back now."

The Celarans calmed. They flashed at each other for another second, then they worked together to carry a flat hexagonal plate up into the air. They headed for an exit.

"We spooked them," Caden said.

"Follow them to their home," Telisa said. "I want to know where and how they live. Then get back to the shuttle."

Reconnaissance only.

Caden knew that was the mission, but he had hoped that somehow they would make contact, anyway. The Celarans did not look starved, though he reminded himself he probably had no idea what a starving Celaran looked like; would they shrivel up and move slowly?

"Even though the vines are very sickly, they must be able to find enough food?" Caden asked Lee.

"Most have died, and these will refuse to have children until the situation has improved," Lee said. "Though they suffer, I don't think they're in imminent danger."

"As long as the Destroyers don't come back," Siobhan added grimly.

"Their work under the light of the star is done," Lee said.

The Celarans flew faster than Caden and Siobhan could move, but the attendants and Lee followed easily.

Their destination was over two kilometers away, where they entered the husk of a building missing most of one side. A patch of healthy green vines had been braided across the hole in the side of the building to form a makeshift wall. The Celarans flew toward the wall and slipped straight through, using gaps Caden could not see.

"Wow. I think they used a couple leaves as a kind of door," Siobhan said.

Caden nodded. "That's likely their hideout. It must have taken a lot of work to weave that wall."

"A vine is a joy to work," Lee said. "A day at most. The real work here is that those vines are green and healthy. Perhaps they made a filtration system to protect their vine."

"Should we send an attendant in?" Caden asked.

"No," Telisa said.

"They may have to keep moving," Lee said. "As the vines dry, a feeder moves on. They would not dare drain them too far, or the vines would die. If there are more than those three inside, they would have to be nomadic."

"What now?" asked Siobhan.

"Drop your sap containers for them and come back to the shuttle," Telisa ordered. "Then proceed to location two."

Caden located the shuttle on the tactical and let his link plan a route back. Siobhan took out a pair of transparent sap bags and placed them atop a ruined vine. Lee flew over and attached a tiny balloon with a fingertip-sized light beacon to one of the bags. The balloon inflated with a light gas, pulling the beacon upward.

"I'll set the beacon to start flashing in fifteen minutes. That should give us time," Lee said.

Caden had been told that the beacon flashed a message in Celaran that said more help was on the way. The PIT team was not on a mission of mercy, but if they determined that the Destroyer threat was gone, he assumed

18

Telisa would have the other Celarans and the Space Force come to evacuate the survivors.

"Destroyer!" warned Lee.

Caden and Siobhan both abruptly knelt down behind a ruined vine branch. At the same time, Caden got a report that Lee's forward attendant had died. He found a video feed that showed a glowing ovoid. The breeze picked up.

"Is it a tank or a drone?" asked Siobhan.

Caden understood her confusion. The machine glowed, but it was darker and quieter than Destroyers they had seen, and it was about twice the size of a drone. They remained under cover.

The Destroyers know about Celaran stealth tech.

As Caden prepared to use his laser, he realized the other half of his predicament.

I need a projectile weapon.

The Destroyers knew energy weapons well and had defenses against them. Since their creators were aquatic, they made less use of projectile weapons. Caden decided to use his breaker claw instead.

"Disengage!" Telisa ordered.

"It's only one Destroyer," Caden said. "We have to save those Celarans!"

Telisa did not reply, probably to avoid any more traffic that might reveal his location to the Destroyer.

"Only one?" asked Siobhan. Her tone told him she found his assertion overly optimistic.

Caden watched the tactical map in his PV. Lee flew away from the Destroyer, either in fear or obedience to Telisa's command. The attendants were also withdrawing.

"Maybe if I shot the building it would scare the Celarans away," Caden sent to Siobhan privately. Since she had covered only meters from him, he figured the communication would not be noticed.

"Shoot the Destroyer," she said. He smiled.

She's with me on this.

"You use your claw, I'll try my laser," she said.

"No! You'll give yourself away."

Siobhan's forward attendant went off the tactical. A second later, the vine before them flashed into flames. They dove away.

"It can already sense us!" she said.

Good point.

Caden sent her a nonverbal acknowledgment along with the signal for "open fire".

His lead attendant hid under a stunted vine leaf the size of a dinner plate. It spotted the Destroyer and routed its location onto the tactical. It was only sixty meters out, coming around the building where the Celarans had been working.

So close already! Good. Within breaker range.

Light flashed across the sickly vine field. Caden's stealth suit indicated it had protected his vision from a dangerous energy spike. He told his claw to activate on the enemy target.

Booom!

"Got it!" he transmitted, then debris started to rain down.

If those Celarans are still around, that'll get them to flee in short order.

He looked over and saw that Siobhan's echoform had a flashing red arm in his vision overlay.

"Siobhan!"

"I'm okay," came a distressed reply. It sounded very much *not* okay.

"You're hit! Can you get your medikit? I'll cover you."

There were no enemies on the tactical. Caden inched over in case Siobhan had been disabled and needed help getting the kit in action. At the same time, he told one of the attendants in his stealth envelope to go and join his forward one to watch for other Destroyers.

"I can do it," Siobhan said.

"How bad?" asked Caden.

"Those Celarans are long gone, you hear me? Get out of there," Telisa ordered. She sounded angry, but Caden remained focused on Siobhan and did not process it.

"My hand is gone," she said. "I think my laser gave away my position."

Her hand! Gone!

"It burned the vine right in front of us before we attacked!" Caden protested.

"Yes, but it missed. I don't think it knew exactly where we were." Siobhan was already moving again, though slowly. Caden delayed a few seconds, watching the tactical, then he retreated after her. They had three kilometers to run to the ship, so he had plenty of time to worry about Siobhan's arm and meeting Telisa when they got back.

Lee doubled back to fly closer to them. Caden forced himself to pay as much attention to the video feeds in his PV as his injured friend. If another enemy appeared, he would have to react quickly to protect her.

Caden had rotated through all the views and returned to the tactical when he noticed Siobhan had stopped. He turned to view her silhouette through the cloaking system. She had fallen.

"Siobhan!"

"I'm... coming..."

No, you're not.

Caden turned and walked up to the edge of her stealth envelope. He had never done that before, even in virtual training.

"Uhm, Lee? Siobhan needs help. Is there any reason I can't go in there and carry her? Does one of us need to deactivate our cloaking or anything like that?"

"The vines can twist and tangle. There is no harm," Lee said. "I'll watch the underleaves."

Caden walked over to Siobhan. She had collapsed near one of the colonies of red grubs. Caden suppressed an urge to deactivate their stealthing and make sure none of the insects had gotten onto her.

Just hurry.

Caden told his suit to release a strength enhancer into his bloodstream and scooped Siobhan up into his arms. Between the drugs, the weak local gravity, and her light frame, it felt like he carried a hollow mannequin.

Low gravity girl, he thought. *I can do this.*

Caden started to run. He selected a weaving course through the low vines. The attendants left alive behind him had not detected any more dangers. Slowly, the load he carried started to feel heavier. Caden found himself breathing hard.

"Are you there?" Caden asked Siobhan.

"Yes. Are we going to make it?"

"Definitely."

Telisa met him halfway. She took Siobhan without a word and bounded away. Caden heaved and puffed in his suit. The cooling had kicked in, but his muscles ached even in the low gravity.

Before Siobhan left his link range, he asked her suit for the damage assessment. The report he received indicated that the trauma was limited to one arm. The suit had stabilized her.

She'll be okay, he told himself. *This time.*

Chapter 4

Siobhan lay on a medical web in the top-of-the-line medical bay of their new *Iridar*. She tried to hide the discomfort of having an artificial left hand attached to her recently destroyed lower arm. The automated medical machines had quickly removed the burned flesh, fabricated a hand and wrist, and attached it to her body. The hand twitched as it trained to understand her motor signals.

Telisa stood by the webbing. She had not said much; Siobhan knew Telisa was displeased with their decision to fight. Caden had been denied entry into the med bay and told to prepare to back up Lee and Cynan on the second half of the scouting mission.

"I might be of use—" Siobhan started.

"No. Stay there," Telisa said. "You're on pain meds, your body took a shock, and besides, that hand isn't fully trained to your nerve signals yet."

She knows me well. Forcing me to sit here while the rest of the scout mission goes on is truly awful punishment.

"You can watch the feeds," Telisa continued, adding a slight tempering to the sentence. She turned and walked out. The only company Siobhan had in the bay were the clean white structures of the medical machines and the one-armed remains of her Veer suit, hanging nearby like a spectre sent to remind her of the injury.

The silver lining was that their new ship had a better med bay than the PIT team had seen since the *Clacker*; it was equipped to regrow limbs. A round white bin with three green lights blinking on its surface hummed quietly from across the room as it grew her new hand. The link interface said it would take days or weeks, depending on how urgent she was to reattach the replacement. The longer she waited, the stronger and more capable her new hand would be, though once attached, it would even longer to regain coordination.

Siobhan accessed the video feeds from one of the six wide ramps of their new *Iridar*. She saw Caden standing a few meters from the ramp, in a gliding suit, with a Celaran lift rod strapped onto each limb. The arrangement might still leave him more sluggish than Lee and Cynan, but at least the gravity on Celara Palnod was relatively weak. His face looked worried.

"What's up?" Siobhan asked. "Mission too tame for you?" she teased on a private channel.

"I'm good. Are you still in pain?"

"I'll be fine," Siobhan said. "This artificial hand already feels fairly steady, and we're growing a new one."

In truth, her lower left arm ached where it had been burned away despite the drugs running through her blood. Her hand worked well, though not perfectly. The medical bay programs had told her it would adapt along with her own brain until her full dexterity returned. Then she could start all over again with a real hand.

She saw Caden nod in the video feed.

He blames himself. Or he's put off about Telisa's reaction to our decision to fight the Destroyer.

Surprisingly, Telisa had delayed meeting with the team about recent events until the second half of the scouting mission completed. Siobhan reviewed the shared team plan in her PV. Cynan and Lee would be going out to get a closer look at the larger Celaran-like creatures that inhabited the planet. Caden would be trailing them at a distance. Siobhan could not tell if Telisa's decision to hold Caden back was practical or emotional. It certainly made more sense for the natural flyers to monitor the high-altitude creatures, but making Caden hang back could also be Telisa's way of expressing her displeasure with his actions.

Siobhan spotted the two Celarans already flying above the natural support spikes and their load of sickly vines with green trunks and reddish leaves. They ascended in a gentle spiral course. The star's light shone down with only a few clouds to obscure it, and the temperature was pleasantly warm by Terran standards.

"Stay sharp. We don't know what these other... Celarans are like," Caden told Lee and Cynan.

He's worried these mutant Celarans could be aggressive.

Caden used his lift rods to take off after Lee and Cynan. He pumped his limbs to help generate lift and save some of the equipment's energy. He activated his cloaking sphere and disappeared. His echoform was lost in the light of the sky for a moment until it switched to a dark color for contrast. After that he was easier to see, but the view was not nearly as interesting.

Siobhan switched her attention to the tactical in her PV. She also saw the targets on the tactical: the unusual Celarans. She checked their altitude. The creatures were gliding about three kilometers above the forest canopy, just above one of the only clouds in the sky. Suddenly a question came to mind.

"Are Cynan and Lee armed?" Siobhan asked on the team channel.

"They have lasers," Telisa told her. "We also have six attendants up there with them that could accomplish a lot, defensively or offensively."

Siobhan considered that. The attendants could fly well, even as well as Lee, and if they decided to collide with a target, it would hurt. Siobhan supposed an attendant could even hurt a Terran through a Veer skinsuit if it had enough space to take a long run at them. The Celarans had no such body armor. They preferred to remain light and agile to avoid any conflict.

"How can these groups survive the Destroyers?" Siobhan wondered on the channel.

"I doubt they could," Caden said. "I noticed that they stick close to the clouds. Either they need the moisture or they're using them as cover."

The tactical showed Cynan and Lee nearing the aliens in the cloud. Caden remained over a kilometer away. Siobhan's interest became sharper. Her two Celaran teammates chose a group of two targets on the flank of the larger flock.

"Lee and Cynan can handle the initial approach. Caden, hang back and cover them," Telisa ordered.

Caden sent a nonverbal acknowledgment. He lowered his airspeed and let Lee zip toward the strange Celarans.

"I have an idea about these Celarans," Caden said while he waited.

"Tell us," Telisa said.

"I think they come from another colony. They adapted themselves to a slightly different environment by making themselves larger and wider. They must have come back to visit the homeworld and found this... or maybe they're searching for survivors?"

"An interesting idea," Telisa said. "Where are their ships? Their rescue equipment?"

Caden did not answer.

It occurred to Siobhan that their ships could be cloaked in space or on the surface of the planet, but she had no theory about the absence of equipment and supplies.

"There are too many here for them all to be visitors," Cynan said. "The population is in the millions in this starlit sky."

"But Lee said they wouldn't have children in these circumstances. So they couldn't have been born here," Siobhan said.

Lee's marker came within 50 meters of the alien creatures and held the distance. An attendant advanced with Lee, obscured by the cloud. It rose slightly above the moisture and got a high-quality feed of the creatures. The wide Celarans soared majestically, peacefully, seldom changing course and proceeding without urgency.

They're happy doing what they're doing. These creatures aren't panicked or desperate.

Siobhan saw the two wide Celarans glowing. The colors cycled too fast for her to sense any patterns.

"Are they speaking?" Telisa asked.

"Yes!" Lee said. "They're talking about the wind."

"So they speak the same way you do. But when you left this planet, none of them existed?" Telisa pressed.

"That's right! They're new leaves on the vine. I can understand them, but they do speak differently..."

"How?" Siobhan asked.

"They speak simply."

"Well, there's nothing complex to talk about here. Maybe they live a more primitive life," Siobhan suggested.

"Perhaps it is so among the clouds," Lee said. "Do you want me to talk to them?"

Will Telisa dare to let Lee show herself? Surely we could protect her from those Celarans...

"No. Release the collector bugs."

"Won't they be terrified by those things showing up at this altitude? And hitting them?" Siobhan asked.

"I hope they'll find it curious, but nothing more," Telisa said. "We only need a few cells. Then we can understand them better, discover their origins."

But we could also learn so much by talking to them. Surely Telisa will see that soon. We've lost a lot of people, but isn't talking to Celarans relatively safe?

Caden launched two collectors. The tiny machines whizzed off rapidly. Siobhan fidgeted uncomfortably as she watched them close, wishing she was up there flying with the team.

The collectors made their pass. Each one zeroed in on an alien. The Celarans reacted with startling speed, splitting and dodging away, but the machines were faster. Siobhan could not follow exactly what happened, but the targeted Celarans folded up and dove toward the ground. Siobhan's breath caught in her throat. It was as if two light gauze kites suddenly turned to lead and plummeted. The collectors reported success.

"Are they okay?"

"They're startled as if the predator struck from underleaf. But under the light of the star, they seem fine," Lee said.

"It was only a mild graze, just like before," Telisa said.

Siobhan saw that the two Celarans had pulled up from their dive, moving in different directions, using the cloud as cover.

"Good job. Return to the *Iridar*," Telisa said coldly.

All three members of the aerial team sent back nonverbal acknowledgments and turned for home.

***

When Telisa finally called the post-mission meeting, Siobhan was ready to face their leader's wrath. Telisa arrived in the mess hall with Magnus at her side, looking all business. Magnus was unreadable. These were the undisputed leaders of the team. Siobhan missed Cilreth, who had also been a part of that group. In that moment, she felt bad for being impatient with Telisa for being so cautious: they had lost so many from the PIT team.

It's happening to me. I'm getting older and I've seen enough bad things happen that I'm losing my fearless streak. I promised myself that would never happen, but I see it now.

Siobhan was actually about the same age as Telisa, but she had not been there on Thespera 2 when Jack and Thomas died. She had not gone through the terrors the others had faced on Shiny's homeworld, or the battles with the UED.

"So we've learned a bit about two groups of Celarans that still live here," Telisa summarized. "Unfortunately none of them appear to be advanced enough to help us. Rather, the Space Force and our other Celaran friends will have to come rescue them."

Everyone absorbed that without comment.

"What went wrong on our first mission?" Telisa asked.

"We failed to remain hidden and ended up in an engagement," Siobhan said. "However, I think it was the right thing to do, given there were innocents who could have been killed had we done nothing. It was a lone Destroyer."

"Three things," Telisa replied firmly. "First, those Celarans have been avoiding the Destroyers here for a while now. They're smarter than those war machines, and I bet they've learned a lot about avoiding them."

Siobhan and Caden nodded. Marcant and Magnus remained impassive.

"Secondly, we didn't know it was alone. I agree, however, that Destroyers we find around here probably will be remnants that are likely isolated since we have not detected any Quarus ships or bases here."

Telisa paused again. Siobhan waited for the last point.

"Third, follow my orders unless you're certain I've made a miscalculation, such as if you know something out in the field that I'm unaware of. I'm monitoring the attendant feeds, the map, and the channels. I'm making the best calls available to keep everyone safe, but all that means nothing if you won't follow my lead. Siobhan, you could easily be KIA right now. That weapon could have struck you dead center and turned your torso to ash instead of your arm. The Destroyer must have been unable to lock on to you in the cloaking envelope, but you're still left with only luck to protect you."

Siobhan knew Telisa was right. Yet she felt she had only acted to protect those poor Celarans.

"Does anyone have any suggestions or training tweaks we should adopt while we consider our next mission?" Magnus asked.

"Our weapons were not optimal for an encounter with Destroyers. We should have seen that coming," Siobhan said.

"Are you trying to pick a fight with her today?" Caden asked privately.

Marcant almost said something then, but apparently, he decided to leave it alone. Siobhan suspected one of his AI friends had just told him to keep his mouth shut.

"Our breakers saved the day," Caden said. "But they can't hit a target kilometers out like our projectile rifles can do."

Telisa nodded. "We'll adjust our weapon selections. Magnus and Caden, at least, will have long-range projectile weapons on them. When we next deploy a team, we'll have a more complete arsenal."

"What are the chances that the Destroyers here are also programmed to target Vovokans?" asked Marcant.

"Well, that Destroyer did shoot at the attendants, but I assume you're suggesting we make better use of the battle spheres," Telisa said.

"I hope you'll consider it. Why toy around with dangerous Destroyer machines when we can utterly stomp them?"

"The plan was to go unnoticed... but I suppose that has less viability than I had hoped. The Quarus have learned to find cloaked Celarans and designed their Destroyers accordingly. I guess we'll deploy the battle spheres as backup from now on."

Telisa looked at Caden and Siobhan.

"If you encounter Destroyers, draw them into the spheres' line of fire. Put in some VR practice with that in mind."

"What are we doing next?" Marcant asked.

"We'll continue to search for information about those who left this place," Telisa said. "If we can't find any leads, we'll have to try another system."

"It's a sad thing to hide from these sap suckers," Lee said.

Siobhan followed her meaning.

"I know," Telisa assured Lee. "It seems like we're not helping them, but we could only feed a handful. By coming here and scouting the situation, we not only open the way for more aid to come from the Space Force, we can also try and find the other factions to reunite your race. Trust me, our actions will benefit them, all of them."

"The starlight has only shown us those without joy," Lee said. "I think maybe those who left the vines behind have not returned."

Siobhan was afraid Lee might be right.

Michael McCloskey

Chapter 5

Magnus held Telisa in his sleep web. They hung naked in the middle of the room in a tangle of arms and legs. Telisa kept shifting her limbs the way she always did when she could not relax. Magnus knew her mind remained active, examining her problems over and over.

"That was an unbelievably bad call to send the team out with only lasers and breakers," Telisa said. "Of course there would be Destroyers left patrolling around, equipped to defeat Celaran stealth technology and harder to kill with lasers."

"I guess I failed to take your mind off your work," Magnus said with faux hurt in his voice.

"If I had made the obvious connections—"

"Mistake made. Mistake corrected. Lesson learned," Magnus said. "We've always carried a wide variety of weapons, and that's the best choice out on the frontier and beyond. It serves everyone's personal preferences, and it gives us diversity of firepower."

"I also should have had Siobhan and Caden on the same page about contacting the natives directly from the get-go."

Magnus breathed deeply.

Damn. Now I'm thinking, too. So much for relaxation.

"Marcant's with us on staying out of contact, but the rest of the team wants to talk to these Celarans. Well, I guess I don't know what Cynan thinks," Magnus told her.

"Our mission isn't to save the Celarans here one by one," she said. "We have to find other fragments of their civilization."

"But most of the Celarans fled the planet, right?"

"Yes, they may have. I hoped to find scouts who had returned, or other installations with clues about where they may have gone."

"Trying to find those clues may be a tall order," Magnus said. "We have a whole planet to search..."

"But wouldn't they have left messages about where they were going?"

"Not if they were afraid the enemy might find the messages and pursue them."

"The Celarans are good at hiding. There could be a few advanced hideouts down there that the Destroyers never found... let's take a week. If we don't find anything by then, we should move on," she said.

Magnus relaxed again. Telisa rested her head on his chest and he stroked her silky hair idly. He felt utterly content.

A notification from his link interrupted his moment. *Damn.*

"What is it?" she asked, sensing his tension.

"A search report came in and got flagged by some filtering rules I set."

"Then we have a lead!" She slipped out of the web and started to put on her Veer suit.

"Potentially," he said lazily.

He felt tired, but he knew host-body Telisa did not really need sleep, though she could attain it if she tried.

He closed his eyes and focused on his PV. The planetary map showed Magnus everything they had found: flocks of the large, dull Celarans and the scattered oases of healthy vines where many Celaran survivors had gathered. He reviewed the list of interesting sites cataloged by the automated search so far. He found the report that had been flagged and studied it.

"Electromagnetic anomaly. Probable large power source. No Celaran infrastructure detected. Unusual vegetation patterns present."

"I'm going to send attendants to investigate a site," Magnus said.

"Sounds good," Telisa said. "I have some things of my own to check on."

She walked out of the room. Magnus dispatched a group of attendants to the site. They would take a couple of hours to arrive at normal speed.

Just enough time for a nap.

***

Magnus awakened to another link notification. He stretched in his sleep web. A ship's service told him he was alone in the room. He accessed his PV without opening his eyes. He saw a report that told him his four-attendant team had arrived at his mystery site. He connected to the feed and started watching their progress.

He saw the vines had grown in clearly artificial patterns. He saw an overall pyramidal shape with many oval extensions at various levels of a massive, healthy vine system. Large tunnels opened in the leaves at regular intervals. He struggled to make sense of it. The place had the feel of an ancient site of religious significance, not a modern structure.

It's a huge vine... temple. Maybe it's been preserved as a historical site?

Two attendants split up and entered two different tunnels while the other two flew up and over the entire structure. Inside, he saw square walls formed by vine stems and leaves. The plants were amazingly dense and flat, as if they had grown up against invisible force fields. He had an attendant push on a nearby leaf. It deformed as they attendant pressed against it. When the attendant retreated, it resumed its perfect shape.

No invisible walls. Just disciplined vines.

Magnus switched out to an external view. The temple grew almost 400 meters high, and the attendant had not identified any underlying frame other than the natural support spikes far below. Magnus knew the support spikes never grew anywhere near that tall. He sent the other two attendants into the mass of vines to search for hidden supports.

The feed skipped. Magnus felt confused for a moment. Then the feed resumed, but the healthy vines were gone. The attendant feed showed a 360-degree view of the sickly red vines.

What happened there?

Magnus flipped through the other attendant feeds, and then their histories. They had all suddenly skipped. Magnus checked the tactical.

The attendants he had sent to investigate were scattered across the continent. None of them remained at the vine temple.

Instantaneous teleportation. I'd say we have something here.

"Hrm. A mystery," Magnus sent to Telisa.

"What do you mean?" she asked on the channel.

"There's definitely something weird going on at that site," he said.

"Please tell me you have a lead on the cyborgs," she said. "We haven't found any operational spacecraft down there."

"This," Magnus said. He sent the pointer to Telisa and Marcant.

They studied the EM readings and the strange vine patterns for a moment. Marcant was the first to respond.

"Why don't we send attendants to check it out?" asked Marcant over the new channel.

"I did. They got displaced," Magnus said. "They pop back up kilometers away from there in an instant."

Telisa came into the room. He could tell he had piqued her interest.

"We've seen that power signature before," Telisa said.

"How do you know? I didn't find any hits on it."

"This *Iridar* doesn't know about it," Telisa said. "But our original one did!"

Magnus looked over the readings.

They do look familiar! The first Iridar... what does she mean? Oh!

"The Trilisk facility on Thespera Narres!" Magnus exclaimed.

"Yes."

"Not exactly what we were looking for," Marcant said. "Intriguing though, isn't it?"

"Yes. I wonder if the Celarans were aware of it," Telisa said. "Maybe part of the team, absent myself of course, should go there and check it out."

Magnus nodded. "There could be another AI there," he said slowly.

Telisa smiled. He had read her thoughts.

"It could be critical. We could use it to oppose Shiny."

"How? Would we have a chance? And is it really our fight?" Marcant asked.

"We can figure all that out later, but we have to balance out the power. It's too dangerous. If Shiny decides he doesn't need Terrans' cooperation anymore, then he could do anything."

"He's given us a long leash. Longer than the UNSF would have, the old one, I mean," Magnus said.

"He took you away from me," Telisa said sharply.

Magnus knew it was time to stop playing devil's advocate. Telisa was not in the mood for brainstorming right now.

"Okay, then. We'll get a Trilisk AI and make sure that doesn't happen again."

"Let us get back to you, Marcant," Telisa said. He dropped from the channel.

"You and I can talk about it some more... later," Telisa said aloud. She approached the sleep web and removed her skinsuit. The structure rotated as Telisa entered the web and took a position above him. Magnus welcomed another pleasant diversion.

Chapter 6

Telisa lay alone in the sleep web by the time a link alert came in. She asked the *Iridar* to explain the alert. A series of panes opened in her PV.

Another ship. Where?

The *Iridar* believed they had been contacted, but Telisa could not find the evidence in her personal view. She missed Cilreth. Surely her old friend would have been able to explain what was going on in a matter of seconds.

A channel request came through to Telisa. The metadata displayed a warning in red: "Caller is a duplicate of locally known link ID for Telisa Relachik."

Telisa had only a second to understand what that meant, then the other Telisa spoke.

"Another me? I guess I shouldn't be surprised. Though I didn't expect to see any other Terrans out this far, much less myself."

"Where are you? Cloaked?" Telisa asked.

The other PIT team members tried to connect to her. They must have realized something unusual was happening. For the moment, she sent nonverbal stand-by replies.

"Yes. This is a Vovokan ship," Telisa9 said.

The ship finally showed up on the Terran *Iridar*'s sensors. The other PIT members redoubled their efforts to connect to Telisa.

"Stay calm, I'm talking with them," Telisa sent to the PIT channel.

Regular life is hard enough; now I have to deal with this? She paused to force herself to take a different attitude. *This is me. An ally, not an enemy, so relax. I need all the allies I can get.*

Telisa recalled the last time she had met a copy. "Have you been on Skyhold?" she asked.

"What? No. Is that a test question? I don't know the right answer."

A different one.

"I was just curious if you're the one I've met before. We're here to find Celaran refugees," Telisa said. "What's your mission?"

"I guess we're off mission, actually," Telisa9 said slowly. "We were investigating some Talosian ruins and came across a Vovokan robotic exploration vessel. It knew about aliens living here, so we came to investigate, but it looks like catastrophe has struck."

"I can tell you what happened," Telisa said. "Let's meet FTF, as disturbing as that might be."

"Yes, let's meet."

Telisa considered the possibility that this was a trap. Whose trap could it be? A Trilisk? They would have to carefully check for signs of Trilisk activity. Shiny? If it was something Shiny had engineered, she did not need to worry about giving away mission details. They might not want to mention any thoughts about resisting him, though...

"Who's on your team exactly?" Telisa asked as she thought it through.

"We have myself, Arakaki and Maxsym," her counterpart said. "We lost the rest."

Telisa could hear the pain in her voice. Telisa added a video feed of herself to the channel and Telisa9 returned the gesture. She looked at herself. The other stared as if afraid to speak.

When she hears about Magnus... by the Five. She's already waiting for me to say...

"Magnus is here," Telisa blurted. She watched her twin's face freeze to hide the reaction that could not be hidden. Telisa knew exactly what her other self felt. She had been without Magnus for a long time before, but he had been returned to her.

"This is very sudden—" Telisa9 stammered.

"We also have Siobhan, Caden and Marcant. We lost our Cilreth in a battle with the Destroyers," Telisa said.

Not to mention a lot of others we've lost.

"Ours too... though it wasn't Destroyers. It was horrible," Telisa9 said. "I've never heard of Marcant."

"I guess he's too recent. He never worked with the team during the time we had the Trilisk columns with us."

"Then maybe he's never been duplicated at all," Telisa9 finished.

"So Shiny has sent out other teams led by my copies," Telisa said. She realized her blunder after she had spoken. She shook her head. "Oops, sorry, I'm a copy too, a Trilisk host body like you."

Telisa9's mouth opened slightly and her face darkened.

Something's wrong.

"I'm not," Telisa9 said slowly. "I mean, a copy, yes, but I'm a normal Terran."

"How's that possible?"

"Shiny has learned how to copy us as ordinary Terrans. It doesn't have to be a host body anymore. Besides, Magnus led our team... he was..." Telisa9 faltered.

Telisa anxiously swallowed, waiting for her to continue. The dread was palpable.

"Magnus was a host body. Shiny did that to cement his place as the leader. But we came too close to a living Trilisk... It was days before we even knew. He took out half the team." A tear ran down Telisa9's face.

Telisa absorbed that. It was not easy, and she had not even lived through it.

She was broken.

That scared Telisa.

"We have safeguards in place, early warning signals to alert us of Trilisk activity."

"So did we," Telisa9 said. "But we were out on an expedition far from the ship. When the Trilisk took him, it must have learned about the detection. It was able to remotely sabotage the warnings."

By the Five.

"I'm willing to share him with you," Telisa said quickly. She did not have to say who she meant. "Shiny took him off the team for a while... I know what you're going through. Well, kind of. I always had hope of getting him back."

Telisa9 did not say anything. Telisa knew it was because she could not refuse the offer, even though she also felt wrong about accepting it.

"We'll talk about it more in a few minutes. Come over to this ship?" Telisa asked.

"Yes..."

She's thinking about what to say to Magnus. Or whether to avoid him altogether.

"Just to calm some nerves, we'd probably better exchange attendants first and scan each other for signs of Trilisks."

"Go ahead and send one over when we connect," Telisa9 said. "We won't. I know now that given sufficient warning, Trilisks can easily avoid giving themselves away."

Of course. They are Trilisks, after all. Stupid of me to think we had a guaranteed way of detecting them.

"It's not that bad, I think," Telisa9 said. She must have been able to read her own face. "I think they usually do show themselves. It's only if they know we'll be looking that they might suppress all the normal signals, if for some reason they find themselves at a disadvantage and want to hide."

Which they usually don't.

"Let me tell my team what's going on," Telisa said.

"Of course. We'll all be there soon," Telisa9 sent, then disconnected.

Michael McCloskey

Chapter 7

Magnus waited for Telisa's report with great concern. The seconds seemed to stretch forever. There was another ship out there, and they had no idea where it was. That meant they could be destroyed at any second.

"We have visitors. Very special visitors. Marcant, get our Trilisk countermeasures on a hair trigger," Telisa ordered.

She wants us on high alert. And that command just accomplished it most effectively.

Siobhan was the first to ask.

"Aliens? *Trilisks?*"

"Another PIT team," Telisa answered. "They've had exposure to Trilisks."

Oh. That. And they ran afoul of Trilisks.

Magnus checked his weapons.

Where did I leave that special gas grenade?

Magnus searched through a wall trunk filled with gear. He did not find what he was looking for: a grenade that would dispense Maxsym's deadly anti-Trilisk gas.

Of course. Lost it on the other Iridar. I should have brought it with me everywhere.

Magnus steeled himself. He knew the "original" Telisa was in a column somewhere, so if his current Telisa was ever taken over, he should not hesitate to kill her. Even with that in mind, he felt serious reservations.

"If I do anything amiss or we detect any signs... you know what to do," she sent to the team channel.

The other ship uncloaked. The sensors told Magnus it was a Vovokan ship. It closed on the *Iridar* and prepared to connect to it. He walked over to the lock. When he met Caden there, Magnus opened a private channel to communicate to Caden silently.

"Even if we get the all clear, stay wary," Magnus told him. "I'll lead them to the mess, you take the rear."

Caden nodded. He did not complain about the plan to treat PIT members as potential enemies; he had heard the warning about Trilisks the same as everyone else.

The lock cycled open, exposing a Vovokan connector tube that joined the ships. Magnus heard footsteps approaching. He had his rifle ready to fire, though lowered.

The first person through the docking tunnel was a large blond man: Maxsym. He did not appear to be carrying a weapon. Though Maxsym looked similar to Magnus in complexion and size, his skillset and demeanor were much more peaceful.

"Clear," Marcant said on the team channel.

Magnus walked forward and offered Maxsym his hand. Maxsym shook it firmly, but the look on his face was not pleasant.

"Magnus. Very good to see you... again," Maxsym said tightly.

"And you, Maxsym," Magnus said sincerely.

What's wrong here?

A short, athletic woman with black hair and distinctly Asian facial features walked out next. She slowly nodded toward Magnus. He dipped his head in return.

Arakaki.

"She's clear, too," Marcant transmitted. "Though she's stressed out. On edge."

Well, she's walking into strange ship filled with other PIT teammate copies... but it's more than that, isn't it? She's upset like Maxsym.

An attendant passed Magnus and headed into the tunnel.

Magnus felt a little awkward standing beside these ghosts. He imagined it was worse for Caden, who had almost worshipped Arakaki. Another Arakaki.

The real awkwardness began when Telisa9 walked out to join them all. Her beautiful green eyes glanced at Magnus and then darted away.

Oh, wow. She looks rattled.

"None of them are Trilisks," Marcant said on his PIT team's channel. "I've sent an attendant into the connector tube as well. So far, all clear."

"Welcome to the *Iridar*. Our *Iridar*, I mean. We can talk in the mess," Magnus said. He did not want to turn his back on them, but he thought they might feel the same way. He fell in beside Maxsym and walked them toward the mess, letting Caden take the rear.

Unless he's distracted by Arakaki, of course... stay paranoid, stay alive.

Maxsym's eyes wandered, examining the interior of the ship.

"Is this of real Terran make, or is the Vovokan getting better at making ships for us?" asked Maxsym.

"Yes, it's Terran-made, though Shiny's been sharing some know-how with the Space Force. Weapons especially, to help against Destroyers."

"I'll just pretend like I know what Destroyers are," Maxsym said. Magnus decided to wait to comment on that until they were all together.

Caden offered his view to Magnus's link, understanding that it might be tactically useful. Even though no fight had broken out, Magnus accessed the view and saw that both Arakaki and Telisa9 watched him carefully from behind, though perhaps for two very different reasons. Arakaki looked ready to put a bullet into him in an instant's notice, while Telisa9's gaze was more forgiving.

They arrived at the mess. Siobhan, Telisa, and Marcant awaited them. Lee and Cynan had made themselves scarce.

"What's your mission here? You're saving aliens?" Maxsym asked.

Magnus thought that Telisa had said she already told the other Telisa the basics, but he supposed Maxsym might just be looking for details.

Telisa saw she had the attention of the other three PIT members, so she let them have it with both barrels.

"The Quarus built robot weapons called the Destroyers. They decimated Shiny's homeworld. These are the aliens that destroyed the *Seeker*. They sent Destroyers to inflict genocide on the Celarans as well. This was the Celaran homeworld."

"By the Five..." Telisa9 whispered.

Maxsym's face also showed surprise. Only Arakaki did not respond, except to shift her weight from one leg to the other. Magnus noted Arakaki had a stubby submachine gun hanging at her side. The other guests had only laser pistols.

Well, at least she's not a Trilisk.

"I'll send you pointers to the details on the Quarus and the Celarans," Telisa told them.

"I look forward to seeing some in person. Well, Celarans, at least. Do you have any samples?" Maxsym asked. "I'd like to take a look right away."

Magnus recalled that Maxsym had been the team's xenobiology expert. He smiled, anticipating Telisa's next revelation.

"I neglected to mention, we have two Celarans on the team," Telisa said. "Sorry about holding back on you, but we all had a lot to absorb."

"I want to meet them!" Telisa9 said immediately.

Maxsym brightened. Even Arakaki started to look around as if searching for the aliens already.

"Lee?" Telisa signaled.

Lee and Cynan made a dramatic appearance, flying in from the far door. Lee looped and swirled, excited as always. Cynan remained more stationary, with his silvery body hovering a meter above the floor.

"Amazing!" Maxsym breathed. "Are the differences in their appearance related to sexual differentiation among Celarans?"

"The vines twist and turn, but their leaves all grow alike," Lee sent to them. "My species has but one gender."

"Cynan is a cyborg, is all," Magnus clarified.

Maxsym walked forward, delighted to examine the aliens. It looked funny to see such a large man as excited as a young child at a party.

Caden, Siobhan, and Lee started to fill Maxsym in on the details of Celaran physiology. Lee basked in the attention happily, flying in acrobatic patterns and hovering before Maxsym. Magnus looked over at Telisa9. She and Telisa had moved away to talk between themselves.

***

"There's something we need to talk about," Telisa9 said. Telisa looked at her and nodded so she would continue. Telisa9 walked to one side, drawing her away from the main group in the mess.

"We have a Trilisk column on our *Iridar*."

"What? Well—"

"We don't have control over it, Shiny does," Telisa9 explained. "We use it for our brain state backups, that's all."

"I'm surprised he would part with one and give it to your team."

"New development. He's figured out how to create new columns using the AI."

"By the Five! He can do anything now."

"Anyway, I know Magnus and the others are in there. But only Shiny can use it."

"And he'll only do that if you bring him something good."

"The Talosian expedition was a wash," Telisa9 said. "I think that civilization went dark aeons ago. There isn't much left. I wonder if they were wiped out suddenly and utterly. Bottom line, no great tech to learn from, no answers. Just very old ruins."

"So you decided to come to this place," Telisa finished.

"Do you have anything that would convince Shiny to make another Magnus? Do you have any tachyon communications set up?"

"No. Well, not yet. We're looking for more Celaran allies."

"Then I don't know what to do," Telisa9 said.

Have I ever looked that sad and broken? Telisa asked herself. *Maybe, but only in front of Magnus.*

"If only we could control that column. Our software expert, Marcant, managed to gain control of two Vovokan battle spheres. But I can't imagine he will able to do the same with a Trilisk column."

Telisa9 nodded. "There's a possibility that the real columns contain the consciousnesses of Trilisks. Some of the columns, at least."

"You mean backups?"

"No, I mean active beings. Not necessarily awake or paying attention to the... 'real' world, though."

"Wow."

Telisa thought about the columns she had seen. The first group had been on T2. Had there been real Trilisks watching her even then? Or were the aliens so busy doing something else that they had not even noticed her?

"Maybe some of the Trilisks aren't against us," Telisa said. "Maybe they helped in ways I'm not even aware of."

Telisa9 tried to smile. "You still have the old optimism."

"How did you lose yours?"

"First Shiny betrayed us all. We had a fruitless mission, and then on the way back, Magnus turned. When the bad things cluster, you see how little control you have over anything."

"Hang in there. We'll get you patched up." It felt strange to say to herself, but it fit.

"Seeing Magnus is freaking me out," Telisa9 admitted. "Half of me wants to hug him and half of me wants to shoot him."

"This Magnus is not a host body, so choose the former."

***

Caden and Siobhan retreated to his quarters after talking to the remnants of the other PIT team for an hour. Eventually, they could not tolerate Maxsym's inexhaustible curiosity, but left Lee to it, since she seemed happy to answer his every question. Meeting the other team had been a strange experience, but Caden decided they would be better off to have more highly skilled people on their side.

"You're still all messed up about Arakaki," Siobhan said.

Oh, no. Here we go...

"No, *you're* messed up about her," Caden replied.

"When she's in the room, you stand straighter and stop talking to me on our private channel," Siobhan said.

"I..." Caden's voice trailed off. "Yeah, it feels weird. But I never slept with her. So don't act like she's some old flame, okay?"

"If I was your second choice—"

"Not at all! You know what we have is special."

"Then what's your deal with her?" Siobhan asked. "Don't sugarcoat it."

"I admired her skill. And I was so surprised to find out I could work with a soldier from the UED! They were the bad guys, the enemies of the Space Force. When I was a kid, we would play VR games all the time with everyone split into two sides: UNSF and UED."

"Go on."

"She really opened my eyes. I had been so Space Force centric. Telisa and the PIT team started me thinking about my blind loyalty to the UNSF. I had doubts about this job, you know? Until I saw Arakaki and how she cooperated with us for the greater good. Now, it's just strange because she died to save my life, but today, there she was, standing around like her death was just a VR exercise."

"She's just another copy," Siobhan said.

"Same woman, though."

"Okay. You get to work with her again. We can both learn from her. Just stop making it weird, okay? Get over it."

"I will. I *have*."

Caden's eyes slid away from Siobhan, and he forced himself to accept the weird nervousness in his gut.

I am so not over it.

***

After the excitement died down, Magnus remained with Telisa in the mess. Arakaki and Telisa9 had returned to their ship after catching up with Caden and Siobhan. Eventually Maxsym had left as well, speaking of his plans examine their data on Celaran physiology.

Caden had been acting weird, but Magnus figured the young VR champ would work through it. He wondered if Caden and the last Arakaki had hooked up before her untimely death. Did they share memory of that? It would be enough to make things awkward.

I'm sure Siobhan noted it, too, he thought. *Ah, young drama.*

Still, the meeting had brightened the mood on both teams, though clearly the magnitude of the information hitting the other PIT team had sent them for a loop.

"These two teams need each other. We each replace missing pieces of the other, except for me. There are two of me," Telisa said.

"Telisa, you don't have to take them on," Magnus said.

"Yes, we do. They also have a Vovokan ship. We need that ship, too. The other Telisa and I will figure this out. We'll make it work."

"How? It's going to be—"

"We made it work for Cilreth. Besides, Terrans need to get used to this technology. The UN government is gone, at least in the Sol System. This is going to happen."

"I'm sure Shiny will keep that on lockdown for his own use," Magnus said. "It's another edge he'll be happy to have over the competition."

"We'll see what we can do about that."

Magnus placed his hand on the edge of the sleep web and started to slip in. Telisa grabbed him by the arm and held fast.

What's this?

"I told her you'd visit her," Telisa said. "These are her quarters over on their *Iridar*."

She sent Magnus a pointer to the ship map Telisa9 had shared with her.

Uhm. I guess Caden and Arakaki don't have the market cornered on drama.

"'Visit'?" he echoed.

"You know."

"I have a say in this, too," Magnus said.

"Get in there and sleep with me. That's an order," Telisa said in a playful voice.

Magnus tilted his head and looked skeptical.

"Yes, really," Telisa said more softly. "Today it will feel strange, tomorrow—well, next week, anyway—it will be the new normal. That's how it was with Cilreth's copy."

"I never got *that* used to it."

"I know myself. This is temporary. She'll go back to Earth when she gets the chance and have Shiny make her a new Magnus from that column."

"Then she could wait—"

"Don't be cruel. Try to shut down any guilt reaction she has. Please, don't pretend like this favor I'm asking is unpleasant."

Magnus opened his mouth, expecting another protest to emerge, but he found he had no argument to offer. Instead, he just exhaled and accepted it.

"I'll see you later," he said.

Magnus accessed the map and slowly walked out.

Okay, that was a first.

Chapter 8

Maxsym felt very satisfied with the current mission. He enjoyed sneaking around, spying on new lifeforms, and snatching a sample here and there. On top of that, for every sample they collected, he could spend dozens of hours scanning the molecules and setting up the analyses to show how they worked.

He could clearly remember his first mission with the PIT team on the space habitat. After that, he knew that events had occurred for which he had no memories. Eventually, he had been assigned to a PIT team and sent out again.

The last mission had not provided much stimulation. There were a few tiny bits of alien flora and fauna to learn from, but they had all been simple things. Most of his time over the last three months had been spent trying to understand the wonder that was a Trilisk host body. For all his work, he had only managed to comprehend a few short splices which might have been the primitives of the most sophisticated dynamic genome imaginable.

Maxsym's latest analysis of the high-altitude Celaran forms had been loaded into his simulators. The genetic differences were very clean and localized. Clearly the result of external design, and yet the biggest of the splices had already been seen.

"Curiouser and curiouser," Maxsym said aloud in his Vovokan lab. He brought up a pane in his PV about the familiar segment that had been introduced into the larger Celarans.

Ah, yes. This makes sense. I should report this immediately.

"Telisa?" he sent. Then he realized he had connected with *his* Telisa.

"Yes?"

"I've finished my analysis of the samples taken from the large specimens," Maxsym said.

"The wide ones? What have you learned? Wait. Let me get my copy in the loop."

Maxsym saw that the other Telisa joined the channel. *Strange days...*

A second later, Caden and Siobhan connected. Maxsym gave anyone else who might have been notified a few more seconds to join, then decided to start.

"These creatures' genetics are determined by a four-branched tree of long strands of—"

"Four? Does that explain why their young are the product of genetic information from two, three, or four parents?" asked Telisa.

"What?" Maxsym gasped.

"I may have forgotten to mention that," Telisa said apologetically.

"Yes, that explains a lot," Maxsym said and halted to think.

"I'm sorry. Please tell us what you learned."

Maxsym took a deep breath.

"I see evidence of genetic manipulation in both our 'normal' Celarans and these larger ones. In summary, my theory is that the Quarus poisoned the vines, so the Celarans moved some of the vine processes into their own bodies. This large subspecies is producing the same sap provided by the vines within their bodies."

"Photosynthesis?" asked Telisa9.

"An equivalent chemical ladder," Maxsym said. "Their increased size is critical. They need to gather water vapor from the clouds and then catch a larger cross section of starlight to produce what they need. These Celarans were designed to survive *here*."

"That's amazing. In fact, too amazing. Wouldn't it have been easier to fix the vines instead? Create a version

that's immune to the poison, or filters it out?" asked
Caden.

"Maybe it's one of several parallel lines of research,"
Siobhan said. "The oases might be the result of new types
of vines that were designed. If your entire race is dying,
you don't put all your hope into one fix, right?"

"Also, some of the spacefarers fled," Magnus said.
"Groups like Cynan's cyborg mixes. Others stayed. They
used multiple strategies to survive."

"So this is one solution. Apparently a relatively
successful one. They've adapted to the changes in their
homeworld."

"This group, anyway," Maxsym agreed. "Remember,
this group is only large compared to those that stayed here.
I hope, for their sakes, that the majority managed to flee
the planet."

"The solution will be short-lived if the Destroyers
come back to finish the job," Magnus said. "I hope the
Quarus only wanted to knock the Celarans down until they
weren't seen as a threat."

"What kind of race could see the Celarans as a threat?"
Siobhan asked.

"It doesn't matter. We'll take the war to the Quarus, if
we can. In the meantime, the Celarans can decide if they
want to leave their homeworld and join the Space Force on
the new colony," Telisa said.

"How?" asked Maxsym. "As advanced as the genetics
of these amazing creatures are, they seem to live primitive
lives now. I doubt they can help fight the Quarus."

"Yes," Telisa agreed. "First, we need to verify that the
anomalous site Magnus found is Trilisk."

"Oh, no. That's the worst thing we could do!"
Maxsym blurted. As soon as he said it, he felt embarrassed
at the obvious fear in his voice.

"Easy, Maxsym," Telisa said. "I'm not going
anywhere near that place."

Michael McCloskey

Maxsym nodded. He relaxed a little.

"Still... we need to put our Trilisk protections on high priority. We need to work together to improve our measures in case I become a mind slave."

"I'll see what I can come up with," Maxsym said.

And whatever I devise will be my secret, so that a Trilisk wouldn't find out from you.

58

Chapter 9

Arakaki chewed on the sliver of her ex's armor. It was not the original, but neither was she, so it did not bother her. The new unified team had just finished a round of training, and Arakaki found herself alone in her quarters. She did not feel like sleeping, so she listened in on the team channel.

"It's definitely a Trilisk facility," said the stranger named Marcant.

At first she was not sure what he referred to exactly, but she saw a location get updated on the planetary map in her PV. She zoomed in and saw an unusual vine formation on the surface. Not only were the vines healthy there, they had grown into unusual geometric patterns that reminded her of a primitive temple. A lot of data had been attached to it, including a dozen attendant missions, yet nothing had managed to gain much data on the inside of the place.

"As we suspected. Thanks for the verification. That means I'm out," the host Telisa said. "We all know it's too dangerous for me to go anywhere near there."

Arakaki checked again for Trilisk emissions in the *Iridar*. She suspected the rest of the team was doing the same.

"I can go," Telisa9 said. "You could take a team to investigate another promising site."

Arakaki's mouth compressed into a thin line.

Trilisks.

She remembered all too well what had happened when their Magnus had become compromised. He had torn through the team leaving death in his wake before Arakaki had dropped him with a bullet through the back of his skull.

How many more Terran soldiers are going to die from those damn demons? We should have been fighting them instead of ourselves.

59

"Magnus, Lee, Cynan and I will check out a promising oasis," Telisa said. "We'll find out if any of them know about the factions we're searching for. The normal Telisa, Siobhan, Caden and Arakaki are on the Trilisk site. If this planet has an AI... that could be huge."

"Another trinket for Shiny?" Arakaki sent to Telisa directly. She did not try to keep the venom from her voice. The link message would convey her emotive content perfectly, unless Telisa had filtered it out.

"It's time we took one for ourselves," Telisa replied. "It's the only way we could ever hope to oppose him."

This one is not broken like my Telisa. She's ready to fight back.

Arakaki tried to evaluate how she felt about that. Was she doomed to forever fight a losing battle against the rulers of Earth? First Terran and now alien? She chomped on the fragment in her mouth.

It doesn't matter. I'm going to keep fighting. There's nothing else for me to do...

Meeting the fragments of the other PIT team had gone over smoothly for her. There was a time when she had just wanted to die, at least as long as she could take the Konuan with her. Now, the prospect of living many lives brought mixed feelings. It seemed like maybe she would never die, which meant she would always feel the absence of her one real partner in life. On the other hand, her pain had finally started to fade. She was no longer fighting a losing war in an environment where she could only remember what she had lost. The enthusiasm of the PIT team invigorated her. She felt her zest for life returning.

"Okay, get to it," Telisa ordered.

Arakaki accessed the data that many Terran and Vovokan machines had gathered on the mysterious location on the surface of Celara Palnod. The site was only a few square kilometers of land tucked away between two hills, but the vines grew so thickly there it reminded

Arakaki of a jungle. The leaves were enormous, over a meter wide, and unlike the other regions she had seen, the flora here looked perfectly healthy. For the first time she was able to imagine what this planet must have looked like before: a lush paradise.

Arakaki, Siobhan, Caden and Telisa9 grouped up on their own channel to confer on the new mission.

"The vines here are abnormal," Caden was saying as Arakaki connected.

Arakaki saw only deep green, healthy looking vine branches and leaves from the first video feed she reviewed. She kept watching as they talked.

"Not normal being not poisoned? So you mean abnormal for this planet?" asked Arakaki.

"Here's an analysis of the stems," he said. A new pane became available in Arakaki's PV. She focused her attention on it.

A complex but regular pattern had been superimposed upon the view of the site. At first, she thought the lines represented an artificial structure under the vines. As the image rotated, it became clear that the regular lines were the vine branches themselves.

"The vines are not growing randomly here," Siobhan said.

"Yes. This is a design," Arakaki said.

"This structure was *grown*. It looks like some sort of temple," Siobhan continued.

"Interesting you should mention that. Wasn't Earth's AI located in an underground temple?" Caden asked.

Siobhan invited Lee to their channel.

"Lee? Did you know of this place before the Destroyer attack?"

"A place as ancient as the vines," Lee sent back. "Primitive Celarans came here and forced the vines. It was strange, but it was their way."

61

"Did they worship someone or something there?" Siobhan asked.

"Their ways were strange and are forgotten like yesterday's starlight. We do not build vine structures this way any longer."

"Totally forgotten? It's important. Was there a religious sect?" Siobhan persisted.

"They thought the planet was alive," Lee said. "Not the vines, but their roots. Or the crust of the planet itself. That is all I know."

"Thanks, Lee," Caden said. Lee dropped from the channel quickly.

"Is she always like that? Seems like she thinks it's a waste of time," Arakaki said.

"Celarans are very playful and seem to live in the moment," Caden said. "But yes, she clearly doesn't care about those who used to live there."

Arakaki's video recording of the scout suddenly dropped out.

Something got the attendant at that point.

"Do each of these feeds end the same way?" Arakaki asked.

"Yes. We don't have any idea how they get kicked out," Siobhan said.

"There's not even any death rattle info," Arakaki said.

"Well, yes, they didn't die. They were teleported out. We haven't seen what does it," Caden said.

Okay, this could be my shortest mission yet. That I can remember.

Arakaki finished examining all the information they had gathered. There was not much to go on, just the video from attendants that had been moved, orbital scans, and the weird power readings. She accessed more files available to the team about the Trilisk complex that Magnus and Telisa had encountered on Thespera 2. It looked like the Trilisk outposts were usually underground, contained the columns she had seen, and often found in round tunnel complexes that could not be scanned.

No wonder Magnus and Telisa are so close. Their relationship was forged in fire.

Arakaki realized her stomach was growling. She headed for the mess of the Vovokan *Iridar*, then, on a lark, she headed through the connector over to the Terran starship. She went to the alternate mess that was not home to the flying aliens.

Magnus sat at a table eating noodles with pieces of synthetic protein on the side of his plate. He had not yet spotted Arakaki from the other side of the room. She slowed and moved softly. It felt good to sneak.

Arakaki considered Magnus solely as a male example of the species for a moment. His heavy frame was apparent even in the Veer suit. She found him attractive and capable. Of all the PIT team, Magnus most resembled her long-dead ex. But like Caden, her other choice, this male had been drawn into an exclusive relationship with another.

What's that saying? All the best ones are taken.

Magnus looked over quickly, presumably just noticing her.

"Did you hear me?" she asked.

"Caught sight of you in a feed," Magnus said, pointing at one of the attendants that orbited him. Arakaki had yet to take any of the Vovokan spheres for herself, though she used them in the VR training.

"You're watching through them all the time now," Arakaki said approvingly.

"It's second nature. Sometimes I dream of what they see. Are you ready to go check out that Trilisk site?"

"Yes. How about your objective?" asked Arakaki.

"Lee can report on the other site. It's a kind of post-apocalyptic Celaran town," Magnus said. He added Lee to the channel. Arakaki felt a little put off. She had felt like talking with him alone.

Is he just trying to be helpful or did he do that to avoid a private chat?

Lee eagerly jumped in at her chance.

"I would be as happy to do so as I am to hang from a juicy vine," she said over the channel.

The alien shared a pointer to a repository of information drawn from their scouting. Arakaki accessed it and saw a Celaran community built on three hills covered in vines. The dwellings sheltering among the vines were so dense that it looked like three complex castles overgrown with Terran vines.

"The local vines as they twist and grow had been mutated as an attraction for travelers," Lee explained. "As the star rotates over the ages, a local tradition kept them this way. These vines are more primitive, less engineered, than those that dominated our planet. Their sap has a unique taste. They were preserved as an oddity."

"And that's exactly what saved them from the Quarus designed poison," Arakaki guessed.

"As correct as feeding from the vine. And where there is sap, flyers aggregate. This community of survivors has only a few thousand individuals, yet this is one of the larger places left. Those who make their lives on these vines have collected a lot of technology from the remains of our civilization. They're definitely not simple minded like the high flyers."

Then why aren't there Celarans feeding at the temple site? Something keeps them away.

"So the hope is, this group may be sophisticated enough to be in communication with Cynan's faction," Magnus said.

"If the Destroyers come back here, this will be a juicy target," Arakaki noted. "Sorry, Lee, I did not mean juicy in the way you would use that word, I think."

"I think I see the twist of your vine," Lee said.

"We're heading out tomorrow, so hopefully we'll be able to find what we need soon. Besides, the Quarus may not return here. This planet could no longer be a threat, even if the Celarans were bloodthirsty," Magnus said.

"And the oceans?" Arakaki asked. "Could the Quarus be hiding there?"

"They might be, but the oceans of Celara Palnod are very shallow compared to Earth and the other planets we visited. Telisa thinks the Quarus don't want this world."

"Purple pasted bastards," Arakaki said aloud, off the channel. "We should be bringing the war to them."

Magnus smiled. "I think that's exactly what Telisa intends to do. She just wants to find a few more friends first."

Michael McCloskey

Chapter 10

The two teams were an hour away from starting their respective missions when Telisa9 came to visit Telisa on board the Terran *Iridar*. Magnus, Lee, and Cynan were also on board, since the Terran commando vessel would be dropping near the Celaran colony to search for clues. Siobhan and Caden had departed to the other vessel which would go to the mysterious vine temple.

They met in her quarters. Telisa9 looked somber.

"Any last details?" Telisa asked even though she knew it had to be more than that. Most things could have been handled over a link connection. Her fellow copy wanted to talk about something important.

"I have to tell you something about your Magnus," Telisa9 said.

Only the Five know... she sleeps with him and now... what?

Telisa9 must have seen the look of pseudo-dread on her doppelganger's face.

"As you know, Shiny selects Trilisk host bodies for the leaders of his teams," Telisa9 began.

"Yes. At least the ones that aren't going to investigate Trilisk ruins, I'm guessing."

"Well, he did more than that. Have you noticed how Magnus has changed? He used to guide you more."

"He was my mentor. But I have more experience now, thanks to him."

"Has he argued with you? Challenged any decisions?" asked Telisa9.

"We... *discuss* things all the time."

"But does he ever really push back hard when he disagrees?"

"What? You're suggesting my Magnus has been... meekified? I think it's just that he knows I'm the leader now. He respects me."

"Of course he respects you. I'm not implying otherwise. But his chemistry has been subtly changed to... *more fully* accept you as the leader."

"Shiny told you that?"

"Not directly. But I've picked up clues. And now—"

"And now that you *slept with him* you discovered that this one's different?" Her voice wavered more than she wanted.

This is insane. I'm getting irritated with my copy.

"He's different than my Magnus was. It's subtle. Maybe you haven't noticed because of all the pressure, everything that's been going on with your team. I can see it because I went straight from mine to yours."

That last part came out sounding guilty.

"So once again Shiny proves to be more insidious than I expected," Telisa said grimly. She had to force herself to continue: "Thanks for telling me."

Telisa9 nodded. "Good luck."

"You too."

Telisa9 left. Telisa thought about her copy's observations.

The other Telisa is also less aggressive than I am. Her spirit is broken. Perhaps Shiny dialed her down, too, since her Magnus was the team leader. Maybe she could not say that herself—if she sees it.

Telisa wondered if there was a team out there with a Cilreth as the leader, or even a Caden. Did Shiny experiment with them all? How could he come to any conclusions when every team faced different challenges? It seemed like he would have to experiment for a thousand years to see any patterns emerge from the chaos of such varied missions.

Maybe he has virtual simulations running on his vast computational systems, trying us all out in different combinations. He might choose a leader for a team based on the mission parameters.

Shiny was not the only one building teams. Telisa herself had made the call on who to assign to each sub-team for the two tasks before them, but more decisions remained to be made. There was Marcant, Maxsym, Achaius, Adair, and their Vovokan battle spheres to be considered.

The battle spheres had very limited stealth abilities. They could change color and move silently, but that was about it. They could not become invisible as the team could, so they should not be with the teams. Normally Telisa would assign the battle spheres to protect the ships and be done with it.

We have two ships now. Losing one would be bad, but no longer disastrous. Losing both is less likely.

"The Vovokan battle spheres will trail us, one for each team," Telisa announced on the team channel. "They can't go in with us, but they'll provide a safety umbrella if we have to retreat. Marcant and Maxsym should stay with the ships."

She received a handful of nonverbal acknowledgments. She ordered a sphere over to the Vovokan ship and checked everyone's location. Once the sphere had crossed over, and everyone was properly divided between the ships, she broke the tunnel connection.

"Good luck everyone," she transmitted and told her *Iridar* to take them to the chosen drop point.

***

Telisa found the Celaran town on the tactical and oriented herself. She stood meters from the ramp outside the *Iridar* with Magnus, Lee, and Cynan. All four of them sent one of their attendants ahead.

"Okay, this will be easy to find," she commented. "They live among only healthy vines around here."

The group had a long walk and fly ahead of them. In order to avoid detection, they had landed several kilometers from the Celaran town.

"Cloak," Telisa said simply. She activated her own cloaking sphere. Magnus winked out of sight a moment later to be replaced by his echoform. Lee and Cynan followed suit.

"Can you hear me?" Magnus asked on the channel. Everyone sent an acknowledgment.

The team moved out. As Telisa walked, she tried to anticipate what could go wrong with the mission. Though Telisa had considered allowing Lee to be seen by these Celarans so she could talk with them, that decision had not yet been made. She hoped they could learn what they needed to know without exposing their presence.

The scouting attendants flew low over the mounds of dying vines, looking for Destroyers. None had been spotted anywhere nearby, but that remained one of her greatest worries. The team had gone out with combined arms this time, at least. Lee and Cynan had laser rods and Magnus carried his projectile rifle as well as his knife and breaker claw. Telisa had replaced her usual laser pistol with a projectile pistol, though her own breaker claw remained her primary weapon in case they faced robotic foes.

Telisa looked back. She could barely make out the Vovokan battle sphere behind them. Its surface mimicked the rotting vegetation behind it. As it moved in front of a patch of sickly red vines, its surface reddened to match the vines it obstructed from her point of view.

She would probably not be able to spot it at any distance without her enhanced host body vision. Would a Celaran notice it? Celarans processed more visual information than Terrans, but their bodies were not equipped with eyes that could focus on distant targets.

They had evolved in dense vine jungles where line of sight never extended far.

"There aren't any Destroyers around here," Magnus said. "Why do you think they haven't found this place?"

"There may not be enough left alive," Telisa said. "Or..."

Hrm, what does he want me to guess?

"Defenses? Traps?"

"Yes. I wonder about it."

"Be careful and look for traps," Telisa said to Lee and Cynan. "We're wondering if the inhabitants of this place have a way to—"

Before she could finish her sentence, an object in the video feed of one of the attendants cut her short. It looked like a giant metal flower resting under a layer of plant debris. The attendant had stopped to investigate it.

"Is that some wreckage?" Telisa asked, tagging it for the others.

"The attendant says it has an active power source," Magnus said.

"It's a tool underleaf," Cynan told them. "Your understanding of Celarans is more advanced than I would have suspected."

I think it's time their language gained a word for 'weapon'.

"Oh, he's just paranoid," Telisa needled. She knew Magnus would smile, though she could not see it.

"I think the traps would only activate if the shadows under the vine leaves were cast by a Destroyer," Lee said.

"I agree, though I wouldn't want to fly over that leaf anyway," Cynan said.

The suspected device was not under a leaf, at least not a living one, so Telisa assumed Cynan had used a turn of phrase rather than made a literal statement. She guessed it was an idiom related to flying over a leaf with a predator hiding underneath.

Marcant's models have learned a lot, but they probably aren't perfect just yet.

"Yes, give this tool's signature to the attendants so they can find a clear path," Telisa ordered. "I agree, none of us should test those things, especially Cynan since he would be the closest thing to a Destroyer in this group. No offense, Cynan, but you're also a floating machine."

"Lacking only the ovoid shape, bright light, and violent wind," Cynan said.

Innocent observations or amused sarcasm? But he said it first: don't risk it.

"I thought maybe Telisa and I would be in the most danger, since we're unknowns," Magnus said. "But I interpreted what Lee said as meaning a Celaran trap would whitelist Destroyers for activation rather than blacklisting friendlies."

"Yes, that is most likely the popular vine," Cynan said. "We understand each other."

Terrans would err on the side of making a weapon too deadly. Celarans think of it as putting responsible safeguards on a potentially dangerous tool.

Telisa had the scout attendants sweep the route ahead a second time. They found more of the devices in various states of camouflage. Her link planned another route, bypassing the dangers and she shared it on the tactical.

"Continue," she directed. She strode ahead to take point. If other types of traps lay ahead, she wanted to be the one to trigger them since she had the best chance of surviving.

The attendants started to spot Celarans as the team walked the last kilometer to one of the three hills that formed the town. The healthy vines that wrapped the settlement were thinner than the ones Telisa knew. She saw longer, teardrop-shaped leaves with light green bodies and purple-tinted tips.

Telisa looked at one of the Celarans from a feed. It was skinnier than Lee. It wore a harness like the other Celarans she had met, and carried two rods.

"They must have some power source, or they would have discarded the rods, right?" she asked.

"The starlight overhead," Lee said. "What more is necessary?"

"Well at least they have that," Telisa said. "They don't have to live in total squalor."

I feel bad saying that. Their lives are much worse than a short while ago.

Her lead attendant passed by a Celaran hanging from a vine as thick as a Terran leg. Its dangling end flipped side to side lazily. The attendant went on.

Telisa came up on the alien. She realized the Celaran was voraciously sucking sap from the vine. She had never seen Lee eat from anything but food packets. For some reason the sight before her felt much more visceral; it was like watching a huge colorful mosquito suck blood from a giant.

Suddenly another Celaran whipped its body across the first one, pulling its proboscis from the vine. They flew away erratically with one chasing the other.

"Did you see that? That Celaran just knocked the other one off the vine," Telisa said privately to Magnus.

"They probably have to feed more aggressively now," Magnus said. "Food is scarce."

They walked by without being detected. She chose a large building ahead and marked it for the others to see. They would investigate it first. She led the way over to the construct. Its pocked surface did not look like ceramic or metal. She did not know what it might be, but guessed it might be derived from natural or artificial plant fibers.

Just outside the old building, two Celarans had landed beside a pile of rods and other unidentifiable equipment that rose a meter above the ground. Telisa held her breath.

So many rods. So many owners now dead. And these must be just a fraction of the local count.

The Celarans were opening the rods. Telisa supposed they might be searching for particular tools manually since many of the power cells might be dead. Or maybe the Celarans were looking for good power cells. She had no idea.

Another Celaran seemed to take interest in the gear. It hovered nearby, doing something with one of its rods in the three-fingered hand at its front end.

The rod flashed. One of the Celarans beside the salvaged gear darted away. The new Celaran flew in and collided with the other. They writhed against each other, rods in each hand. One of them retreated out of sight. Then the newcomer sorted through the pile. It had happened so fast that Telisa felt sure that she would not have been able to follow without her host body reflexes.

"Did you see that? They're *fighting* over that equipment!" Telisa said on the team channel. "Lee, is your group special? Are you and your friends much more peaceful than other Celarans?"

"No, but when the vines are scarred by disaster, those who live among the vines are also changed," Lee said.

"It's true," Cynan said. "We who flit among the vines are known to be molded by extreme stress. We become monstrous. It hasn't happened for hundreds of years, but the Destroyers have brought us to this."

"You had wars in the past? I had no idea," Telisa said.

"Not this strange Terran concept. But in times of great stress from natural disaster or overpopulation, we turn on one another until the numbers that hang from the vines are reduced. It's a terrible part of our distant past I hoped we would never experience again."

Telisa was careful not to reply, but she felt a certain relief to see another piece of the puzzle fall into place.

"So that's what has happened here. It explains the Celaran behavior we've seen," she said privately to Magnus.

"We need to be more careful. You and I should not reveal ourselves to these Celarans," Magnus pointed out. "We can't expect them to react like Lee and Cynan. These are... for lack of a better word, savages."

"Magnus and I are missing a lot of what's being said," Telisa said her team. "We can't read the flashes. It's only you two that speak to us through the link protocol."

"I can send along what we observe," Cynan offered.

"Are you sure? Will you be able to keep up?"

"I'll set it up to happen automatically," Cynan said. "My artificial parts can do this easily."

"Thank you," Telisa said.

Cynan's feed came through to her link. Conversation logs started to fill. Telisa could pick any nearby talk to read through. She scanned through it and saw only mundane chatter so far.

"Where should we go?" Magnus asked.

"Around the town, clockwise," Telisa said. "First trip around is looking for any cyborgs. If that comes up empty, we need to ask about a leader."

"This way, then," Magnus said, taking the lead. As they walked around the old building with the rod pile, Telisa spoke with Lee and Cynan.

"Are you two willing to reveal yourselves and interact with these people?" Telisa asked. It no longer felt weird to refer to Celarans as 'people'.

Hrm. I don't think I would speak of Vovokans that way.

"I will," Cynan said. "Lee can stay cloaked. Why suck on the vine where predators can see?"

"No, we're all on the same vine. I'll fit in better than you," Lee said. "There may not be any cyborgs here anymore."

"Very well, if you want this sap together with its biting insects, then take it," Cynan agreed.

They walked around the worn buildings of the town. The Celarans Telisa saw were sluggish, droopy, and spoke little. It was a sad contrast to Lee's normal behavior. The natives seemed to be sleeping, eating, or collecting and sorting supplies.

No one detected them on their route around the town. The team and their scout attendants did not spot any cyborgs. Telisa stopped next to a huge support spike with holes around its perimeter that emitted streams of clear water. Celarans flitted in to drink from all directions.

I thought they got their water from the sap. But I guess there isn't enough sap for everyone here, so...

"Lee, you're on," Telisa prompted.

Lee faded into existence over her echoform. Within two seconds she was completely visible.

"What now?" Lee asked.

"Help us find the leader," Telisa said. "There would be a leader here, wouldn't there?"

"Yes, likely there would be," Cynan said. "Finding the leader should not be too difficult."

"I can ask," Lee said.

She flitted over to another drinker and flashed away. The other Celaran responded with rapid glowing chevrons, then flew away.

"I know the name," Lee said. "And I have an image."

"How do you tell each other apart?" Magnus asked.

"On a light day or a dark one, everyone's light panels have their own shape and spacing," Lee said. "You can't see it? That's a good vine! Now I can admit, I can only tell you two apart from your clothes, weapons, or link identifiers."

"It's the same for us," Telisa said. "Our faces have slight variations that we learn to discern."

Telisa looked at Lee's image of the leader. The Celaran had no Terran name yet.

"So the leader is this... Leland," Telisa said, pausing to assign a Terran name to the Celaran leader in her link memory.

"Yes. You want to find his vine? It will be faster if you let me fly to find him."

Telisa considered that. How dangerous was the settlement?

"Okay. At the first sign of any trouble, use your cloaking device and come back here," Telisa told her.

"As you say," Lee said and darted off.

"I can also recognize Leland," Cynan pointed out.

"Then look. Maybe you can stay closer to us, though. Magnus and I can't move too far while cloaked, or Lee might not be able to find us when she returns."

"Surely there are some principles they could use to find the leader quickly," Magnus said. "Wouldn't Celaran leaders usually be found in certain places with higher probability than others?"

"You sound like Marcant. Maybe Lee is doing exactly that right now. If we were trying to find a Terran leader, what principles would you follow?"

Telisa watched Magnus's echoform as he thought. The display was not helpful, as it only knew his location. She would not be able to tell if he was pondering or getting ready to take a shot. She supposed the echoform would change if he made a drastic motion—like dropping to do pushups.

"I guess there would be no foolproof way. I'd just look for the best protected and well-equipped place in the town," he finally replied.

"A Celaran leader does not hang from the juiciest vine," Cynan said. "Still, Lee found him."

"Already? That was easy," Telisa said.

"Well, you were just hanging on the vine," Cynan pointed out.

Telisa smiled, even though no one could see her face. "Fair enough. Lead the way, please."

They walked under a slender archway covered with the thin vines. To each side, a carbon-strut tower rose twice as high as a Celaran support spire, though the vines had been kept clear of the structures.

Cynan routed a conversation into the channel.

"We have nothing to offer travelers," a Celaran said. Telisa saw the source field was marked as Leland. "Our vines are overused, and we have only a few power harvesters."

"We're seeking groups of Celarans who left the planet," Lee said.

"Why would I know about that? Those who fled the vine cannot return to feed upon it. They won't come back here. Why would they?" Leland said.

"So you haven't seen any cyborgs hanging from your vines?" Lee asked.

"Oh, I've seen one or two. I assumed they were ones left on an old vine to rot," Leland said.

"What vine did they leave for?"

"I did not see them fly," Leland said.

"So you have no idea where they live?"

"I don't know. They wander the vines. They have no home stem or even a jungle to call their own."

"I fly now. I'll flash you again when we next share the vine," Lee said.

"When we next share the vine," the leader agreed.

Lee flitted away and returned to her hidden teammates.

"So much for that," Telisa said. "We might strike out here."

"We can check the next oasis," Magnus said, staying positive.

"At least he's seen cyborgs here. We've just missed them. We should choose a place where they may have traveled next," Cynan suggested.

Telisa did not want to accept failure just yet. The lack of progress just made her feel more stubborn.

"I have an idea," Telisa said. "Cynan, if you would become visible, too, we can check their reaction to you. And maybe someone would tell you if you have any cyborg friends around."

Cynan appeared where his echoform had hovered a moment before.

"And if this doesn't work to flush our prey from the leaves?"

"We try another of these oases as Magnus and Cynan suggest," Telisa said.

Lee and Cynan floated side by side.

Telisa did not see any large reactions from the Celarans nearby.

They know what a cyborg Celaran is, and they're not surprised.

"Follow me. One more time around the town," Telisa said. She walked with Magnus, still stealthed, while Lee and Cynan floated along.

"We're just parading Cynan around? Hoping for... what?" Magnus said privately.

"A friend of the cyborgs might speak to him," Telisa said.

They traversed half the town without any such event, listening to Cynan's translation service all the while. Then a local saw Cynan and flew by her Celaran teammate.

"Tell <unknown> that the vine is thicker near the base," a Celaran flashed at Lee.

Sounds like Celaran sarcasm. Or insult, Telisa thought.

"I didn't know they talked that way!" Magnus sent her privately. Telisa shrugged.

"Why did you call this cybernetic sap sucker that name?" Lee asked.

"Some vines look the same. Isn't he <unknown>?" replied the one who had flashed the message.

"I'm Cynan," Cynan said. "Is there another like me here?"

"The wind blows the bugs off the vines," came the reply. "Perhaps he will be back."

"Bribe him," Telisa said. "We have power cells, or you could give him some of your sap bars."

"Your words are strange. The translator is not working, I think," Lee said to her team. "If this one could help us, he would. You want me to give him gifts?"

"Back from where?" Lee asked the stranger.

"He always comes from the south flight path over the machines we left to dismantle the Screamers."

A new path appeared on the tactical.

"He lives that way?"

"I don't know, but he must. What other explanation is there?" the native Celaran flew off.

"Okay, we have a lead," Telisa said. "Let's check it out."

The path brought them south until the vines thinned. Telisa took a look from the edge of the Celaran town. The greenish support spikes were almost barren, like the bare tree trunks of a denuded forest. Ugly reddish vines, diseased and dying, clung from the spikes, though they did not manage to climb even half way up their supports.

Telisa sent a scout attendant ahead to check the path.

"We should hide again," Lee suggested.

"Look!"

The attendant spotted something new. Telisa focused on the video feed in her PV. It resembled a Destroyer. Her heart skipped a beat. Then it occurred to her the stranger was more Cynan's size. The lack of light and wind quickly made it clear that it was a lone Celaran cyborg. The team headed down the path to meet it.

When the stranger saw Lee and Cynan, he did not run. When they approached within twenty meters, the other flashed and Telisa heard the translation from Cynan.

"You're not familiar," said the cyborg. "Did you come from space?"

"My vine rested on a colony planet," Cynan said. "I've come back to the homeworld with help for your vinemates."

The cyborgs closed on each other until they were only five meters apart. They grew still, floating calmly above the sickly vine stumps.

"What are they doing?" Telisa asked.

"They have faster methods of data transfer that use other kinds of light that are not seen except with machines," Lee said happily. "Just like your links. It will allow them to become friends much faster, I think."

The stranger was the first to flash again. Cynan's translation resumed.

"This is hard to believe. Can it really be so?"

"It's luck for all who hang from our vine," Cynan assured him.

Telisa got tired of the unknown name; she tagged the alien Undine and shared the name with Magnus.

"Undine?" Magnus queried.

"Well it starts with U like unknown, and, after all, they fly in a wave motion like an undulation," Telisa explained.

"After this, I'm telling Marcant that we need an auto name generator at the highest priority," Magnus joked. They focused on the other conversation.

"In older days I would have trusted you," Undine was saying. "However, now, many of us are damaged by the horrors. It will be difficult to—"

Telisa deactivated her stealth sphere to reveal herself before Undine. The Celaran retreated several meters.

Michael McCloskey

"A threat underleaf!" exclaimed Undine, but he did not continue to retreat.

"This is one of the aliens I speak of," Cynan said.

Undine started to float around Telisa, getting a better look at her.

"Why do you trust this thing of the roots?"

I guess that's what a walking thing gets called around here.

"They have saved a whole colony of us on vines under another star," Cynan said. "These very ones faced the Screamers and broke their parts."

"Really? All aliens are dangerous, then."

"They've come to dismantle the Screamers! They brought many ships. But the Celarans from the distant star seek allies on these vines, allies like us."

"Yes. There are more like us, driven underleaf by the Destroyers. Many more. I'll go to my superiors and deliver your message at once."

"Cynan, please arrange a method to contact Undine in the future," Telisa said.

"I've done it," Cynan replied simply.

Undine turned and headed back the way he had come.

We succeeded. And everyone's still alive.

"Great job! Time to head back," Telisa said. "Just to be super safe, why don't you guys cloak again for the hike back... or the flight back, I mean."

Telisa chose a return path that shared most of the route they had taken on the way in so that they could avoid traps or other unknown threats. She shared it on the tactical.

The team cloaked again.

"We've almost made it free and clear. Let's not mess it up now by getting sloppy. Keep a sharp lookout for Destroyers, and mind the traps. Let's get home in one piece," she told her team.

They set out. Attendants led the way to scout out dangers. Lee followed about fifty meters behind with Cynan at her side. Telisa and Magnus took up the rear.

"We need a name for this faction," Magnus said to her privately.

"What's wrong with 'the cyborgs'?" asked Telisa.

"Vague. How about the Cylerans?" Magnus said.

"Cylerans. Clever, but it sounds almost exactly like Celarans," Telisa said.

"You have a better idea?"

Telisa shrugged. "Hopefully it's just a temporary thing. If the groups of Celarans reunite, then we won't need to name any subgroup of them."

"Yes, let's hope so."

Chapter 11

Telisa9 was still thinking of Magnus when her team debarked. They started in a sea of sickly red vines where the support spikes rose naked far above the leaves. One of her attendants floated upwards and fed her a view over the area, facing their target. The vegetation ahead soared higher, forming a green mountain of oval rotundas and passageways connecting them.

Siobhan walked with Caden. The two formed a sub-pair of the team. It reminded Telisa9 of Magnus yet again. Arakaki walked a meter to their right, silently observing the vines, her weapon ready. In a strange way, Arakaki was like a female replacement for Magnus: always alert and loaded with weapons.

If we had all met at the same time, Magnus might have ended up with her. Though I doubt that would have been an exclusive arrangement. Sharing him with her would have been much more painful than sharing him with my copy.

The group approached the edge of the anomaly and headed straight between two round towers of vines. Telisa9 felt that something was off. It came to her quickly: there were no bugs crawling or flying around.

"Weird," Caden summarized quietly.

"In more ways than one," Siobhan said. "There's much less diversity in the smaller life forms around here."

"Less diversity? I don't see *any* native creatures," Telisa9 said.

"The scans show there are some, just not a wide selection," Siobhan explained.

"There should be Celarans here too, right?" Arakaki asked. "Isn't this an important food source?"

"I'm pretty sure whatever got rid of our attendants flushed out the bugs, and probably any Celarans that flew in," Telisa9 said.

"If the same happens to us, it may be a long walk home," Arakaki pointed out. Telisa9 understood what she was saying, but she planned on having the *Iridar* pick them up if they got scattered across the continent.

The team walked onward. The vine runners grew in dense, flowing lines like metal shavings conforming to a magnetic field. Arakaki led the way into the wide opening of a vine tunnel that gradually narrowed like the mouth of a rectangular loudspeaker.

Telisa9's feet met softer resistance underfoot.

Even the floor is made of vines here.

"How's your hand?" Caden asked Siobhan.

"I'm fine. Stay focused," she replied.

Stay focused. Exactly.

Telisa9 started to review her attendant feeds and the tactical in her off-retina visual space. She divided her attention between what her own eyes were sending her and what the feeds brought in through her link.

"Here's a bug? See that? A big yellow one," Arakaki said. She pointed. Telisa9 caught sight of it, a long yellow thing with four strong-looking jumping legs.

"I wonder what's special about it," Telisa9 said.

"Maybe the... owners allow some symbiotic species to come in here to keep the vines healthy," suggested Siobhan.

"I'm surprised the vines don't need Celarans to survive," Caden said.

"I'm sure that Trilisk technology can get around any problems maintaining the health of the vines," Telisa9 pointed out.

Their surroundings dimmed as they walked into a set of three oval rooms connected by a round tunnel of vine runners. There were no openings for viewing the outside, but Telisa9 saw four alcoves in each room. It gave her the uneasy feeling that guardians had stood there, waiting to attack trespassers.

Caden shined a light into one of the alcoves. It was empty. He lowered the light toward the floor and stopped there.

"The vines are darker at the bottom of the alcoves," he pointed out.

"Lack of light?" suggested Siobhan.

Arakaki knelt down to examine the darker sections of vine.

"Something has hardened the vine integument there. My guess would be that something had been placed there for a long time, but now it's gone."

"Placed there or standing there?" Siobhan asked.

I guess Siobhan finds this place as disturbing as I do.

The last oval room had three exits heading into the vine building in different directions and angles of descent.

"Which way?" Siobhan asked.

"Lower," Telisa9 said. "Assuming we're right about the Trilisk signs, the complex will be below us."

Arakaki took the lead again, choosing the middle tunnel which descended at the sharpest angle. Telisa9 followed her. The light dropped significantly. The vines were twisted very closely together to block out the light, and they were several layers of vine walls into the temple.

Arakaki activated her weapon's light. The tight beam revealed a long tunnel ahead. Arakaki stopped.

"See this? More of the dark spots."

Her light swept downward, revealing the runner-covered floor. Telisa9 saw the spots. The darker areas were almost brown and ridged like the bark on a Terran tree.

"Those are like callouses on our skin. The vine casing is thicker there," Siobhan said.

"They're the same distance apart," Arakaki pointed out.

"So..." Siobhan prompted.

"It's a *path*?" Caden asked.

Michael McCloskey

"What?" Telisa9 asked.

"I think it is," Arakaki said. "Something walks here. And its feet always fall on the same spots."

"Interesting theory, but what gave you that?"

"Call it a hunch," Arakaki said. Telisa9 suspected she was being disingenuous, but she could not think of any reason why.

They resumed their descent. By the time they reached the end of the tunnel, everyone had activated their lights. The team had a fair idea of the layout in this area; Telisa9's scouting attendant had flown ahead to map a large part of the temple. She saw a centrally located line of four large rooms with at least ten smaller rooms placed around the perimeter.

Everyone emerged from the tunnel at peak alertness. Caden turned and swept his light back up the tunnel the way they had come and Siobhan illuminated the ceiling with her own.

Telisa9 looked at the map and matched it to the room. Two small archways led to the left, and the largest archway lay straight ahead. The sweep of their lights revealed the next large room beyond.

"Which way now?" Arakaki asked.

Telisa9 pointed straight ahead. Her scouting attendant had observed an interesting pattern on the floor there. Arakaki and Telisa9 marched through the opening side by side, sweeping their lights in all directions.

The center of the room had a real floor clear of the vines. It was a smooth, round surface of at least 10 meters in diameter. The outside edge was white, but it had a maroon middle with a black symbol in the exact center. The symbol had a thick center band with smaller lines radiating from the edges.

"It's a Celaran. Very stylized, but these small lines are the fingers, see? Three on each end."

Telisa9 saw it. She agreed with the assessment: though the body of the symbol was shorter and thicker than a Celaran, with longer fingers at each end, it was still the basic shape of a Celaran, like a thick backslash with three spiky arms at each end.

"Here," Telisa9 said. "This massive capstone covers the entrance."

"That center part is a separate piece? How can you be so sure?"

"I don't think Celarans are very keen to decorate the ground. They think of it as a dirty place to be avoided. But where there's an entrance to an underground lair, the Trilisks would have been sure to make it special to impress the primitive Celarans."

"There's something dense below it. A hollow cylinder," Arakaki said. "A tunnel." She shared her attendant's analysis with the team.

Telisa9 closed her eyes and concentrated.

Open.

"How will we—" Arakaki started. A grinding noise cut her off. The capstone lifted out of its recess in the floor and floated off to one side, revealing a set of stairs.

"Trilisks," Caden said by way of explanation.

Telisa9 felt awe yet again for a race that could create portals which read and interpret the thoughts of any sentient creature.

Caden led the way down. The bottom of the stairs met a large portal of smooth black material. Telisa9 recognized it as the entrance to a Trilisk tunnel.

"Will the battle sphere fit in there?" Telisa9 asked.

"Yes," Caden answered.

"Then let's send it on in. Sure, we could leave it out here to cover our retreat, but now I'd rather have it ahead of us than behind us."

Arakaki and Caden nodded. Siobhan looked relieved.

Why do I care so much if they approve? I'm supposed to be the leader now, Telisa9 reminded herself. *I wish Shiny had programmed me to become bolder if we lost our leader.*

Telisa9 linked through an attendant sphere outside the temple to the *Iridar*.

"Achaius?"

"Yes?"

"We want the battle sphere to lead us in here," Telisa9 said.

"I'll send it to you," Achaius said. "If there's real Trilisk resistance..."

"I know. Even the battle sphere will be outmatched. We'd still prefer it be there."

"Three minutes," Achaius said.

"Wait here," Telisa9 said aloud. She checked the stairs for dust. A fine layer covered the steps, except for regular marks that had been disturbed.

"Something climbed these stairs, maybe recently. There are clear spots... not every step, though."

The others started to examine the stairway.

"It's a pattern," Caden said. "Two marks on a step, then one mark over on this side, and every third step is untouched."

"Weird. But three feet... guess what that means?" Siobhan said.

"If there's a Trilisk in here, wouldn't it be in a Celaran's body? There wouldn't be any footsteps at all," Arakaki pointed out.

Telisa9 thought she had a point. What had used the steps?

"Wait. If we see a Celaran, should we shoot?" Siobhan asked.

"Absolutely not. Check for Trilisk activity first," Telisa9 said.

"Down in the complex, the detectors will be going bonkers, though, right?" Arakaki asked.

"Uhm, guys, some of my attendants just disappeared," Caden announced. "I have one left here with me."

Telisa9 noticed the same with a shock. All of hers had gone.

"Everyone's," she said.

"I still have one here, too," Siobhan said.

Arakaki looked all around. She had none left.

"Achaius?" Telisa9 sent. There was no reply. Without the attendant outside the temple, she could not reach the *Iridar*.

"Hang tight," Telisa9 told them. They waited by the stairs for the battle sphere, but two more minutes came and went without any sign of reinforcements.

"The battle sphere would have been here by now," Telisa9 said.

"It's not coming. I'm sure it got teleported away from here like our attendants," Siobhan said.

"Keep those ones we have left close for now," Telisa9 said. "Tell them to stop orbiting and stay closer to your body."

Caden and Siobhan complied. Siobhan kept hers near the equipment at her waist, and Caden told his attendant to hover behind his head, nestled near his backpack. The attendants looked out of place once they had stopped orbiting. Telisa9 supposed she had just grown used to their typical behavior. She remembered how strange Marcant's attendant bodies for Achaius and Adair looked when they held position.

"Okay, here's where we go stealth," she said.

Caden and Siobhan had their own stealth devices. Telisa9 had a Terran stealth suit, and Arakaki had borrowed Marcant's device. Telisa9 knew her suit was the weak link in the group, but against Trilisk technology, it probably did not matter. Could they really hope to hide from the ancient rulers of the Orion Arm of their galaxy?

"And if we see a Celaran?"

"You can't shoot unless it shoots first," Telisa9 said. "We can't assume it's an enemy."

Is that order going to get someone killed today?

"The Celarans are already crazy fast in the air... a Trilisk host body would be even faster," Arakaki said.

Do I give up all hope of finding benevolent Trilisks?

"Okay. If we see a Celaran exhibiting any super-Celaran abilities, we'd better shoot first," Telisa9 said and activated her suit.

The rest of her team faded away. They stood in darkness.

"Hrm, with all of us stealthed, we have no lights," Caden said.

Telisa9 added infrared and ultraviolet spectrums to her visual input using her suit visor. Her surroundings remained dim, but she could at least make out the portal.

"Okay, expanding spectrums works well enough to get us inside. As I recall, the tunnels have an impossible kind of background illumination," Telisa9 said. She looked back at the others. Her link placed dim green echoforms over her vision at their positions.

Okay, this is a different problem.

"I can barely see your echoforms, even right next to me," Telisa9 noted. "Remember, if you move too far away I won't be able to see you."

Lee had warned her that the cues the Celaran devices used to keep track of each other were directional and extremely weak, designed to look like natural radiation. She had tried to adapt the Terran suit's method of coordination to the Celaran system, but it would not work completely. It was a good thing, Lee had explained, because if the Celaran cloaking devices told Telisa9's suit exactly where they were at all times, it would degrade their protection to the level of the Terran technology, which was inferior.

"On me," she said, negotiating the last few steps. With her in the lead, at least she knew the others could see her well and she would not have to worry as much about their positions.

Telisa9 immediately felt uncomfortable without other video feeds. They used the attendants to scout ahead in almost all of their training scenarios. Sometimes in simulated battles, she would lose all her attendants, and that represented the majority of practice she had at operating without them.

The round portal at the bottom of the stairs led to a blackfield, recessed about five meters into the tube. She reached her finger through and pulled it back, then did the same with her arm. Nothing.

I hope this isn't another Trilisk hotel. Or zoo. We don't need to get stuck in a maze.

She stepped through.

The other side was a perfect round tunnel of black ceramic as she had seen in other Trilisk complexes. The ambient light was dim, perfectly even, and seemingly without source. She shook her head at the impossibilities that made up ordinary Trilisk hallways.

By the Five. Maybe the tunnel isn't really lit at all. Maybe the tunnel just tells me where it is by putting itself into my mind.

She took an image capture from her retina with her link. She checked the picture and saw the hallway.

Okay, it's real light. I think. I'm like an ant trying to figure out the kitchen counter.

The teams' echoforms entered behind her. She started to walk. Within 50 meters, a fork in the tunnel became visible. Telisa9 chose the left tunnel.

They walked in single file. No noise escaped their dampening fields, leaving the hallway in dim silence.

Telisa9 glanced back. Three transparent green ghosts followed behind her.

We're playing Haunted Trilisk Ruins. Fun and games, she thought drily.

The tunnel changed ahead. Her eyes slowly made sense of it as she approached. It was an opening with a wider room beyond. Telisa9 walked in cautiously. Bluish cylinders ran from floor to ceiling, each over a meter in radius. Telisa9 counted four of them in the hexagonal room, placed near corners with two on her left and two on her right.

No surprise. More Trilisk columns.

"I just had an awful thought," she sent to her team. "What if the column on our ship is already in contact with these?"

"Hopefully Shiny told it to keep quiet. I doubt he really wants Trilisk attention," Arakaki offered.

Caden and Siobhan kept their weapons leveled and their mouths shut, physically and electronically.

If there are Trilisks there, do they see us? Do they care?

The columns were clean and smooth. Their outer casings were shut. It made her think of the first time she had seen them on Thespera. Her excitement from that first time had soured into nervousness; the Trilisks were dangerous, and their columns were unpredictable.

Telisa9 imagined foes hiding behind the columns as she led the way in. So many hours of training and dealing with scenario-surprise generators had left her this way. Caden and Siobhan had the exact same thoughts, she was sure, as they fanned out, one to the left and one to the right.

"Clear on the far right," Caden said.

"I can't see behind these two yet," Siobhan said from the left.

Their voices were quiet, almost whispers in Telisa9's head. She thought about the chain: they whispered in their minds because they were sneaking around, the words transmitted by their links, passed along with emotional metadata to a nebulous Celaran communication system, to be converted to the UNSF inter-stealth-suit protocols so her link could get it from her suit and play it into her brain as whispers.

"No one behind them on your side," Caden said, looking across from his position on the right where he could see behind the columns on the left.

"Same," Siobhan said, copying his check from her side.

"Wait! That's not part of the column, is it?" Arakaki said.

A spot appeared on the tactical. Telisa9 took two steps forward and saw a tall, skinny ovoid that nestled against the back of the column to their right. It was only about a fourth of a meter wide at its equator, but over a meter tall. Telisa9 walked sideways to get a better look at it. The gray ovoid had a protruding ring around the top at about chest level. She saw some panels set into the tip above the ring.

Trilisk robot?

"I've never seen anything like it," Telisa9 said. "You guys?"

"No," Siobhan said. She walked forward to take a look. "This ring has a seam around it. It either turns or comes out, I think."

"Don't pull it," Caden said. "It could be anything at all."

"There's no way to know without trying," Siobhan said.

"We can check the rest of the complex and come back to it," Caden said.

Siobhan's echoform lifted an arm but did not touch the ring. Her ghostly hand ran along the edge of one of the panels.

Suddenly Siobhan dropped to the floor. Caden dropped to help her almost as quickly. Arakaki actually turned her back on the two and raised her weapon, as if expecting an ambush timed to the distraction. Telisa9 would have been impressed if she had not been gripped by the fear that Siobhan might be dead.

Siobhan's echoform twitched unnaturally. Caden hesitated for a half second, then he turned her onto her side to ensure she could breathe. Telisa9 swung the pack off her back and set it down. She dropped to one knee and brought out her medical kit.

"Open a port!" she ordered.

This is the second time Siobhan's gotten into trouble on this planet.

"I can't see anything!" Caden said, though his echoform searched the side of her suit. Caden left one hand supporting her head, and put his other hand where her Veer shoulder port should be.

"Okay, I can feel it," he said.

Telisa9 told it to unlock with her link. With Caden's help, they connected a narrow hose from the medikit to Siobhan's suit port.

"Her vitals are strong. Heart rate and blood pressure elevated," Telisa9 said.

Siobhan's upper body rose. She emitted a whimpering sound of distress. Telisa9 noted her own heart rate accelerating from all the excitement.

"Siobhan. What's wrong?" Caden asked Siobhan.

"No injuries," Telisa9 interjected.

"I saw something. I mean, I *lived* something!" Siobhan said.

"Tell us," Telisa9 ordered, keeping part of her attention on the medikit feed.

Arakaki had remained on guard the entire time. Telisa9 let her teammate continue to watch for trouble and attended to Siobhan with Caden.

"It was awful! Like an alien nightmare. I know, that sounds dumb, even impossible..."

"Not impossible," Telisa9 said. "Trilisk technology can be used to experience the consciousness of an alien. Not that our brains are all that good at interpreting it all, even with Trilisk help."

"What happened in the... dream or whatever?" Caden asked.

"I was some kind of cunning, evil worm! Swimming through water. A tadpole with piranha teeth that struggled to kill and kill—it was a living hell. I could remember killing dozens of others just like myself."

"Just a fight to the death?"

"We were in the water. I was young. I had to prove myself. I had to fight and scheme and surprise and cheat... anything to kill all the others. It was a test. I knew I would only have a life if I made it to... maturity."

"In water, you said," Arakaki probed. "Could it have been a Quarus memory?"

Siobhan shook her head. "I have no idea." She sounded shaken up. "I'm sorry. I'm sorry guys, but this was... *stronger* than any ordinary VR."

"Recover for a minute. The medikit is giving you something to calm you down," Telisa9 said.

"No, I'm... okay..." Siobhan said.

"How could it be stronger than total VR input?" Caden asked.

"I had no sense of my Terran self," she said. "I really was that thing. It was all I was. And I could have died at any moment."

"You were only out for a moment," Caden said.

Siobhan sounded confused. "Not to me, I wasn't. It was hours, at least... what is that, some kind of Trilisk mind trick?"

"Probably," Telisa9 said, trying to reassure Siobhan without really answering her.

"You felt a memory like that once, right? A Trilisk one?" asked Caden.

"Yes," Telisa9 said.

"You experienced a *Trilisk* memory?" Arakaki asked, aghast. "What was it like?"

"I wasn't one being, but three, it felt like. Or there were three parts of me, three *faces*. My body had three sides, and each side had a personality, a purpose. It was something about their war. The war which must have shattered their civilization."

"What kind of enemy could have faced them at their peak?" Caden asked, shaking his head.

They took another minute to let Siobhan recover.

"Okay guys, let's not wait any longer for me. We have a job to do," she said, standing up.

"Move out," Telisa9 ordered. She pointed the way.

They left the pillars behind and moved into another long, dim Trilisk corridor. Everyone stayed alert and in a formation with clear firing lanes. Telisa9 could tell that this Siobhan and Caden had been training as hard as her own team. Except for the lack of attendants, it could have been any of a hundred VR training scenarios.

They had walked over a hundred meters before Telisa9 saw another room ahead. She made out familiar shapes in the distance: Trilisk columns rested within.

Telisa9 was the first to step into the room. She immediately noticed that one of the columns lay open. After two more steps forward, she realized that although an outer opaque cylinder of the column had lifted into the ceiling, a clear barrier remained. A creature hovered within the lit interior.

"Frackjammers," Siobhan exclaimed.

"By the Five," Telisa9 breathed. "It's a Celaran."

It's in stasis, like I was, she thought. *Like the real me probably is back at Sol right now.*

The Celaran within the column was much thicker and shorter than the snakelike creatures the Terrans had become familiar with. It was about a quarter of a meter thick with a maroon exterior. Instead of three skeletal fingers, the alien had three much larger black limbs at each end. Telisa9 counted two knobby joints on each of the half-meter long arms which ended in sharp spikes.

"I guess that symbol on the capstone wasn't as stylized as I thought," Siobhan breathed.

"This creature is much more dangerous," Arakaki declared.

"Could it glide?" asked Siobhan.

"I don't think so," Caden said. "But those long claws... could this be one of those 'underleaf' predators they like to talk about?"

Telisa9 agreed that the thing did not look like much of a flyer, but she believed the powerful spiked arms would have been able to fling that thick body among the vines quickly. She had no doubt that any Celaran caught in its double grip would be in trouble.

"No jaws, at least," Caden said, taking a half step closer.

"Fracksilvers, are you kidding? Those super-fang things in its mouths aren't any better! Looks like it could drain us dry in a minute!" Siobhan said. Her voice wavered.

Telisa9 looked at one of the mouths nestled in the center of where the triple arms connected to the trunk. A hollow mouth part emerged there like a partially retracted fang. Like the rest of the body, it looked stronger and more menacing than any Celaran proboscis.

"No way that thing could get through your Veer suits," Telisa9 said confidently, dismissing the idea.

Get yourself together. Where's my Fast-n-Frightening?

Telisa9 recalled again what it had been like to feel the Trilisk memory. She had vomited afterward. Siobhan just needed more time.

"It's asleep and we leave it that way," Telisa9 continued. "Anything else here?"

They carefully examined the room without touching anything. Caden and Arakaki shook their heads.

"Okay, onward," she said. They left the second column room behind and headed into another tunnel. This time, instead of another chamber, they came to a fork in the tunnel.

"Should we split?" asked Arakaki.

Telisa9 considered the idea. It sounded too dangerous to her.

"We have time. Everyone together. Left," she said.

They headed down the new tunnel. Up ahead, Telisa9 saw a warm yellow glow. She tried to discern more columns, but as they neared, it became apparent this was not another column room. She did not see any dark columns or even the other side of the room ahead. It was something big and complicated.

She stepped forward slowly, drinking it in. First, she saw that the bright room opened up above and below, not just left and right. A clear wall lay straight ahead.

Many clear walls, she corrected herself. *An entire maze of them!*

They had apparently stepped up to the edge of a chaotic underground building. Telisa could see up and down through clear floors. The rooms above and below were not at fixed distances like the floors of a Terran building. Instead, several smaller sub-floors were seemingly random distances above and below them.

Opaque ramps and banks of equipment broke her direct line of sight through the complex. Even the transparent areas became too confusing to understand after four, five, or six clear walls. Everything merged so that she could not tell how far the place might stretch in any given direction.

"Any idea what this is?" Caden asked on the channel. His echoform stood alert with weapon ready.

"None," Telisa9 replied.

"It's like a three-dimensional maze with glass walls," Siobhan summarized.

"Let your attendants go," Telisa9 said. "They might be teleported out, even down here, but it's worth the risk. We need them now."

The two remaining attendants flew forward and found their way through the first sets of open portals through the glassy walls. They started to record what they found and place it on the team's shared tactical map.

"I can see the feeds, but I can't tell what I'm looking at," Siobhan transmitted.

"We have to check it out," Telisa9 said. "For now, maybe keep this exit in sight. I don't want it disappearing on us."

Siobhan and Caden looked back nervously. She knew they were thinking about the Thespera complex simulation where the layout changed, trapping them inside.

They advanced in the wake of one of their attendants. They walked through a smooth round hole in a clear wall out onto a balcony. The view downward was dizzying, though Telisa9 saw opaque ramps and machinery at various intervals below. Ahead, a clear walkway led to a group of transparent rooms. Above, the multitude of clustered rooms connected by ramps and walkways told of the vastness of the complex.

"Which way?" asked Caden. "I can't see any obvious end to this, or anything unique to head toward."

Before Telisa9 could answer, she caught a glimpse of sapphire reflecting through the panes in an attendant feed. She instantly felt a stab of adrenaline.

"Something's moving!" Arakaki barked.

Telisa9 knelt and looked for cover even though she was cloaked. It was a hard habit to break, besides, it was possible that a Trilisk might still sense her. Telisa9 saw sapphiric legs moving. They were part of something larger than a Terran, moving quickly. Several see-through walls separated it from her spot.

"It's a Trilisk robot," Arakaki reported.

"Or a cyborg!" Siobhan said.

There's nothing we can do, nothing we can do... it will be too powerful.

"Spread out," Telisa9 ordered.

"It's getting closer," Siobhan said.

A bluish beam of light zigzagged through the clear walls. Its movement pattern made Telisa9 think it was searching.

Or targeting.

By the Five.

Chapter 12

"[Caution not to disturb the vine] I hope this is not offensive to ask, but are you sure we can trust these Thrasar?" Strongjumper asked.

The team had been invited to meet with the local Thrasar leader. Athet, their contact, had sent them nothing more than a location pointer.

Nalus answered calmly.

"[None underleaf nearby] They have no reason to lie to us. You're potential allies against the Screamers."

The Rootpounders made slow progress through the ruined vine field as Sarfal and Nalus drifted lazily ahead. Sarfal considered the cybernetic Thrasar. They had seemed dull before the Screamers attacked. Now Sarfal saw the value in working harder as the half-machine Thrasar did. Sometimes the universe required more from its inhabitants than feasting and games.

Sarfal watched the inputs from the alien spheres as they had trained to do. It was not far to the base, but they had to watch out for remnant Screamer machines.

It still astounded Sarfal how much they owed the Rootpounders. Without the clumsy creatures from distant stars, Sarfal would be dead and Thrasar reunification would be impossible. And yet their technology seemed to be behind that of the Thrasar. It was only the other alien, the one they called Loud, that possessed comparable tools.

"[Predator underleaf] The Rootpounders think we're flying into the net," Nalus told Sarfal. "That's why they ask so many questions right now."

"[Friends on the vine] Could it be? Are your kind also changed by the disaster?"

"[The season has changed] Changed, yes, but not dangerous under the leaves."

"[A new spot to feed] I think we're here."

Sarfal saw a beacon glittering below. It simply announced, "[Below the leaves] We're down here."

Sarfal hovered lower. It required a brave effort. The ground neared, filthy and dangerous.

"[Which vine is it] It's here? Is it camouflaged, or..." Strongjumper asked.

"[The darkness underroot] It's underground," Nalus told the Rootpounders. 'The darkness underroot' was a phrase of legend for the Thrasar, a deep darkness equivalent to a Rootpounder concept of a place of ultimate punishment.

"[A vine unthinkable] It's logical to hide there, for what could conceive of such a horrible place to go?" Sarfal said.

"[A different leaf altogether] Shiny's race lived underground," Strongjumper said.

"[Dirt covered creatures digging at the roots] No wonder you don't like that one much," Sarfal said.

"[A practical solution] It *is* logical," Nalus answered.

Fake vine stalks pulled away to reveal a black metal disk on the ground. The disk rotated, causing its parts to slide across each other until there was a hole.

I don't think I can go down there... Sarfal thought, then a light turned on below. Sarfal could see it was bright and clean inside. Then the idea at least became contemplable.

"[Journey over mountains to discover new vines] Just think of it as a spaceship," Strongjumper said to Sarfal.

The Rootpounder knew what I was thinking! That one knows us well. As they said, Strongjumper is their leader for more reasons than strength and speed.

Strongjumper dropped inside. She fell like a rock, but her two massive legs absorbed the energy of the fall at the bottom.

That's Strongjumper. Just slam down into the dirt as if it's the ground that will get hurt when you hit it.

Sarfal dove through the opening and flitted around Strongjumper below.

"[Clutching the vine] Do you mind if the others drop an artificial vine and descend on that?" asked Strongjumper.

"[Find the vine you need] Grasp your artificial vines; nothing could be more natural," Nalus told them ironically.

The other Rootpounders dropped a rope and started to climb down as was their way.

A cyborg floated out to greet Nalus and Sarfal. Its silvery body was just like Nalus's, though of course its chevrons were placed uniquely.

"[Welcome to my sweet vine travelers] I am Athet, the leader of these Thrasar who have chosen artificial bodies."

"[Glad for fresh sap] I'm glad to find you," Nalus flashed. "I'm Nalus, and my soft friend is Sarfal. The other told you about these Rootpounders?"

"[A tale of giant vines] Correct, though I only half believed until now. Such beasts! And yet they use tools."

"[The jungle hides surprises] Trust me, they're very clever. They fly the stars as we do. And now, they help us resist the Screamers."

The Rootpounders finished descending as a wide flyway opened up. Sarfal glided forward through the well-lit opening. The scary, pressing walls widened apart to form a large open space like the hollow inside of a building or a star cruiser. Sarfal flew three or four easy loops, getting a good look.

The poor Rootpounders just stomped forward and stopped at the edge of the vast room. They were unable to proceed because the partitions blocked them, as they could not fly to whatever section they wanted to visit. Sarfal saw that Athet and Nalus had hovered near the aliens to console them. Sarfal flew down to join them.

"[Underleaf all along] So this faction of Thrasar never left the planet?" Grimfighter was asking through Nalus's electronic connection.

"[This is only a runner] It is only an outpost of the cyborgs," Sarfal explained. "It's amazing even to me... Thrasar almost never contemplate descending underroot."

"[A new vine discovered] Yes, I didn't realize that Thrasar would ever go underroot," Strongjumper said.

"[A fresh vine] This is a new facility, designed to monitor our homeworld," Athet said. "The design is extreme."

"[Predator!] Five powerful beings!" Strongjumper said suddenly, crouching in fear.

Sarfal darted away in an instant.

"[Predator!] What danger?" Sarfal was not sure what the alien meant; had the translator failed? Yet it was clear something alarming had occurred.

A large object flew by on Sarfal's right. Sarfal twisted in the air to get a nervous look. A silver and black delta-winged flyer hovered high over the floor. It was five times the size of Sarfal. A three-fingered metal tentacle dangled from the front, the only clue it was Thrasar in origin.

That's one of us! Such a large body.

"[Are there predators?] What is that?" asked GrimFighter.

"[The vines rustle] What was that?" Strongjumper asked at the same time.

"[Strongest vines] One of us, with a body made to use tools for destruction as the Rootpounders do," Nalus said.

"[Searching the leaves] That one was different than any of you I've seen," Sarfal flashed to Nalus and Athet.

"[A strong vine stem] We have developed new bodies to face the Screamers," Athet explained.

The Thrasar sent Sarfal a data pod to examine. Sarfal addressed the Rootpounders through their electromagnetic protocols.

"[Serve the vines] Some here are so dedicated to protecting us from the Screamers that they have given up any resemblance to their Thrasar bodies. They take whatever shape they need to defeat the predators that hunt us."

"[A strange thing in the jungle] Intelligent predators," Sarfal flashed.

"[A new vine discovered] That is exactly what they are," Nalus said.

The Rootpounders stood, shifting slowly on their massive legs as was their way. Sarfal was not sure how much they were understanding. Athet decided to address them again.

"[The vine accommodates many suckers] I'm glad to welcome friendly aliens! Why have you sought us out? I've heard bits and pieces but you can tell me yourself."

"[Protect the largest vines] There is a Thrasar colony world, vast, covered with many new vines. A small but growing Thrasar fleet and a large Rootpounder fleet protects this place," Strongjumper told Athet through Nalus's link.

"[News of a distant vine full of sap] Nalus has told us this, and much about you. You think we should abandon this world and go there. It's a tempting idea."

"[Revealed in the star's bright light] We only inform, not suggest. I do hope, though, that we can stand unified against the Screamers. The different factions of Thrasar are stronger together, and if you allow us to be your friends, stronger still."

They always speak of stronger, never of safer. But they are aliens, after all.

"[News of sweet sap travels quickly] We will inform others of the colony that is protected from the Screamers," Athet promised.

"[Acknowledge your ownership of the vine] With your permission, we would leave one of these spherical devices here to communicate with you. Surely we could come to some agreements that could collect sweet sap for us both."

"[I favor this vine] I'll stay here and help coordinate communications," Nalus said.

"[Slight startlement] Thank you, Nalus," Strongjumper said.

"[How many on the vine] Are there many of you here?" Athet asked. "The Screamers may return."

"[Nothing underleaf] We may send a relief fleet here," Strongjumper said through Nalus. "There will be Thrasar ships with them so that you may be at ease on the vine. We hope to assure you that not all aliens are a threat."

"[Thump the vine] We will send the news to our friends in space," Athet flashed.

"[Time to fly] Shall we return? This is a huge glide forward. I'd like to see how the other team fared," said Strongjumper.

"[What plans on a bright day] And you, Sarfal?" asked Strongjumper.

"[Fly on a bright day] We're off together!"

Sarfal flew freely, looping and folding as if all worries had evaporated. Perhaps their homeworld could be saved.

Chapter 13

The sapphire monstrosity's legs pumped unnaturally, bringing it toward them, though by a route Arakaki could not figure through the maze of transparent walls. She accessed the tactical. Fortunately, the attendants had been able to make sense of what they saw through the reflections and refractions to create a map of the passageways at least forty meters around them.

A bluish light flickered through the area. Laser-sharp lines danced across the clear walls where it passed through. The light settled on Siobhan.

"What is that?" she asked, crouching low.

Arakaki traced the alien machine's course and projected it forward.

That will bring it in direct line of sight in just a couple of seconds...

Arakaki turned to bring the machine into her weapon's firing arc, but the thing had already turned the corner.

Hisssss... Crack!

The world flashed brightly, then Siobhan no longer stood next to her.

"Siobhan!" yelled Caden.

To Arakaki, it was as if they had been training in a VR sim and Siobhan had simply pulled out of the exercise.

Arakaki activated her weapon.

BlamBlamBlam!

The rounds seemed to have no effect. The blue light shot out again, searching for her. She rolled aside, around a glassy corner, found her feet, and kept moving.

"Don't let it find you! I'll stall it!" Telisa9 told them.

How is she going to do that?

Arakaki did not waste time wondering. In the next instant, she had a plan.

I need to get around behind it. Maybe if it's focused on them, I can hurt it.

Arakaki only half-believed in her own plan. She knew anything as advanced as a Trilisk machine would likely be aware of everything on the battlefield in all directions for kilometers. But it had proved invulnerable thus far, and she had no better choices.

Arakaki ran around another corner, trying to use the attendant-provided tac map to find a good flanking course. Caden's echoform remained in place. The blue light swept over his position, but he had found a hiding spot behind a large opaque cube.

"Get it together!" Arakaki sent him.

"I'm going to kill that thing and whoever built it!" he vowed.

"Use your breaker claw. I'm not sure Siobhan got a chance to activate hers," Arakaki told him.

Caden's echoform started to move again. Arakaki's first instinct was to remain separated, but then she had another idea. If they could not destroy that machine, maybe one of them could at least get out alive to warn the others.

She used the tactical to find a route to take her closer. She ran down one mostly glass-walled hall and through a room filled with oval pods secured atop thick black stands. The pods were opaque and provided her some cover from the sweeping blue lines. She moved to the far side of the room and looked out the exit.

Just ahead was a smooth ten-degree ramp. Arakaki noticed it was not transparent like most of the nearby walls and floor; it looked like a series of flat copper plates resembling the underside of a brightly colored snake.

Here's to hoping that coloration doesn't mean something bad.

Arakaki charged up the ramp. Caden ran in from a corridor on her left and met her at the top.

"I'll hold it here. Go back to the entrance!" Caden said.

"No you won't," Telisa9 said. The tactical showed her only 30 meters away and closing. "It's coming behind me, when it gets to this intersection, we hit it from three sides. I'll use my laser, Caden breaker claw, Arakaki projectiles. Double check your target blacklists and make sure everyone's on them."

Arakaki nodded and checked. Since the two crews had recently joined forces, it would have been easy for someone to overlook adding the other team members to their weapons' friendly lists. Her weapon was correctly configured.

She looked at the intersection Telisa9 had mentioned. The sapphire machine advanced rapidly. Arakaki saw she had only seconds to sprint into position.

She ran for it. It took her four seconds to get to the corner and another four to set herself. The tactical showed the enemy continued fearlessly on the expected course.

The machine walked forward into the line of fire. Arakaki and Caden were opposite each other, but their weapons' smart targeting would probably be enough to prevent them from hitting each other. The team opened fire.

BlamBlamBlam!

Arakaki's three round burst reported direct hits, but she did not see any damage on the machine. The Trilisk robot emitted another bright flash.

Hisssss... Crack!

Arakaki took a breath.

I'm still here.

Quickly checking the tactical, she discovered Telisa9 had vaporized. Arakaki abandoned her position and ran deeper into the complex.

"Caden, move out of there. Go back the way we came."

The thing had to know where their fire came from. The only choice was to move after every salvo.

Caden moved, but he headed deeper into the complex, parallel to her own course. The two attendants had made themselves scarce; Arakaki could tell where they were, but they had found cover.

That machine doesn't care about them. All the better for me.

She told an attendant to trail the Trilisk combatant and broadcast its location.

"It's ignoring the attendants. Rely on them," she sent.

"Okay, but can we even hurt it?"

"Just because a tank can take a hit doesn't mean it can take a hundred," she replied, though she sounded more confident than she was. "Remember the juggernaut?"

The juggernaut had been a large war machine in one of their simulations. It had been too powerful to face directly, but they eventually learned the way to defeat the scenario was to draw it after one person, allowing another team member to hit it from behind. When it turned to face its new attacker, the strategy called for the roles to switch. Caden would know it.

"Yes. I'm up first," he said. Arakaki had planned to say exactly that, but Caden was already maneuvering to fire on the robot. Arakaki would have to hold her fire and wait to move in.

Caden's avatar on the tactical went to the end of a corridor, opening into a large room, where he set up. Arakaki calculated that the machine would be in line of sight within a few seconds. She had her link show her some options for following the robot assuming it would charge at Caden.

What if it just flashes its light again and he disappears?

Boom.

Caden fired his sniper rifle this time. Her suit detected his laser's follow-up to his shot, a common kill move for defeating armor.

The Trilisk machine still did not appear damaged. The blue light swept across the corridor Caden had fired from. Arakaki caught sight of his echoform through the clear walls as he lunged aside and went prone behind an opaque pipe.

He's good. What was it, the Blood Glades? Too bad this is no simulation.

The sapphire robot advanced. Caden scrabbled away from the pipe and fled. Arakaki sprinted after them. She ran down one clear-walled lane and over a long section of see-through floor. She ignored the dizzying view—a fall of at least three stories yawned under her—and took a tight left turn.

Caden was trapped in a corner. Arakaki charged on, oblivious to her own safety. Her link showed her the fastest way to get a good shot from half a level above, so she bolted up ten shallow steps and practically ran into the copper-colored opaque section of a balcony. She told her weapon to activate as soon as it had an unobstructed target.

Riiiip!

Arakaki unleashed ten rounds on full auto. Then she ducked and tossed her grenade over the edge of the balcony.

The Trilisk machine changed course and headed for her. Arakaki pulled her laser pistol out from her belt fastener and pointed it at the fast-approaching machine, hoping she could take a shot through a clear wall. She had no idea how much of the energy the material might absorb. Then she realized it would probably bend the beam. Her laser was not configured to compensate for that.

Arakaki had lost track of Caden. The Trilisk machine was five seconds away from her. It would turn and come up the same steps she had taken moments before. She looked straight down through the floor. She saw more of the transparent maze of rooms, but they were not close. It was hard to gauge how far the drop might be, but it looked to be over 50 meters.

I'll have to jump over this balcony and hope I can find something to land on closer than that.

She gave herself one second to spot another balcony within a survivable drop range below. She saw none. Then she sprung up and pulled herself over the edge anyway.

Boom.

The shot echoed just as she leaped. For some reason her mind searched for the feeling of a sharp impact, as if she was the target. Then she focused on the nearest balcony she could see. It was too far away; she would not make it.

As if in a dream, time seemed to slow, and Arakaki saw the balcony below *stretch out* to meet her. She reached out and grabbed the edge as it raced up to her. Impact. She grunted, even through the Veer suit. She ignored the crazy occurrence and tried to orient herself. Was the machine leaping after her or trying to find Caden?

She spotted the enemy across a gap from her, moving away, searching for Caden. Arakaki started to set up where she could attack it on the tactical, but she had no time. The bluish light settled on Caden's echoform.

It's going to get him if I don't do something right now.

Arakaki charged out of cover with a weapon in each hand. She focused her projectile weapon on the floor below Caden and fired. Her rounds struck the crystalline material and shattered it, causing him to fall through to the level below.

Light flashed. Arakaki checked her tactical and saw him.

It worked! Caden is still alive!

"Hang in there, I'm closing on it," Arakaki said.

"No... I won't let you sacrifice yourself again!" Caden said.

"What?!"

114

"Siobhan is gone... this time it's going to be me!" Caden said. "Get out of here!"

"What are you doing?" she sent. She did not receive confirmation of the transmission.

Caden appeared on the tactical around the corner. Arakaki sent one of the attendants to the area ahead.

Caden's bluish echoform leaned against the wall. He started to run—*toward* the machine.

Hisssss... Crack!

Caden disappeared from the tactical.

What the hell... was he talking about something that happened with a different Arakaki?

Already the blue lines were scanning through the complex again, looking for another victim.

Just let it get you.

Arakaki chomped down hard on the sliver of synthetic armor in her teeth. Something inside her was just too stubborn to give up without a fight.

She moved away from the blue robot, once again heading deeper into the clear maze.

The machine no longer moved straight for her. Arakaki wondered if it had somehow lost her. How could that be? It had been able to flush them out to this point.

Arakaki thought she knew the answer.

It's toying with me. Like the Konuan.

Arakaki expected that at any moment the mysterious blue light would lock onto her, revealing her position, then she would die like the rest. But it continued to probe in other directions. An attendant had dropped off the tactical.

Arakaki got a glimpse of the blue robot through several of the transparent walls. It moved more deliberately now. Its bluish beams continued to search.

Of course! It's having a harder time finding me because I'm not transmitting to anyone.

The Celarans used tight directional signals to communicate from within the stealthing spheres.

115

Somehow, the Trilisks could sense it. Arakaki switched her comm system into a passive mode to stop routing signals through to the surviving attendant. It would give her a chance to survive. She could still see the position of her enemy since the attendant trailing it was broadcasting its location in all directions.

Arakaki walked slowly down another clear corridor. She paused behind a skinny metal tower because it was one of the few opaque things nearby. The half-meter wide tower had rows of vents on its side that emitted small puffs of white gas. Whether it was steam or something else, she had no guess. A glassy wall separated her from the tower, so she did not worry about breathing whatever the mist was. After a pause, she continued.

Lights moved through a large room ahead. Her first instinct was to avoid it, but she saw the light was not like the blue scanner. Red and green hues glowed in varying intensities, but they were not coherent like the sapphire robot's apparatus.

There was no direct route through. Arakaki looked carefully, trying to choose a path that might lead her in. Without the attendants to make sense of it all, it was slow going. She got caught in a corridor that veered away, so she turned back. She saw the blue lines in the distance, cutting across several levels ahead and above: the robot was not far.

Arakaki found her way in through an almost invisible side opening in another clear corridor. The glowing red and green light came from a sphere floating in the center of another half-transparent room. She stopped to stare.

The sphere revolved slowly. Thin hexagonal rods lazily extended and withdrew from its surface. Some of the rods were longer than the radius of the sphere; Arakaki stopped trying to make sense of it. The thing could have no mechanical explanation, at least not in three dimensions.

If I don't make it out alive, that alien might remake me, but I won't remember this.

There were still an attendant on the tactical. It sent its position to Arakaki, but she did not return the favor. She noted that it was closer to the entrance of the maze. Perhaps the Trilisk robot would be distracted for another couple of minutes...

Arakaki sent a short burst to the attendant, noting the presence of the AI and ordering it to return to the *Iridar* with its information at all costs.

Suddenly the Trilisk machine came up an opaque ramp right in front of Arakaki. Already the blue beam neared her position.

What?!

Arakaki realized it must have understood that its position was being broadcast and had somehow jammed or destroyed the real signal and replaced it with its own. She had completely fallen for it.

Please just let me die for good this time.

The sapphire machine rounded the corner.

Hisssss...

Michael McCloskey

Chapter 14

The small crew was in a good mood as they entered the Terran *Iridar* and closed the hatch behind them. Magnus stayed near Telisa in a cargo bay while Lee moved deeper into the ship. Cynan had chosen to stay behind with the others like himself.

A mission completed without bloodshed, Magnus thought. *We could use more of these.*

"Marcant. Report," Telisa said over the team channel.

"The ship is secure. None of you are Trilisks," Marcant summarized happily.

"Good to know," Magnus commented.

"Any news from the other team?" Telisa asked.

"No."

"Can you find their *Iridar*?"

"It hasn't moved," Marcant said.

"And the attendants that went with them?"

"Most of them were kicked out, except two. We lost contact with them as soon as they entered the vine temple."

Except two. Those may have been destroyed. The team could be in trouble.

"Well, the blocked comms is to be expected from a Trilisk facility," Telisa said. "Did the attendants show up at new spots like before?"

"Yes. Also, the team called for a battle sphere, but it was teleported out. Before you ask, they were calm when they asked for it. It wasn't an emergency situation."

Telisa was silent for a second, then she nodded.

"No reason to panic," she said. "They're just taking longer than we did. Still, that call for the sphere means they were concerned about something. Bring us up out of here and closer to the other ship. I'll ask Maxsym if he's noticed anything."

"Will do. What happened with the cyborgs?" asked Marcant. "Did Cynan decide to stay with them?"

"He did. They said there are many more of them who escaped the attack. I think this will be critical. They possess amazing technology and they're ready to fight."

"Doesn't sound like Celarans to me," Marcant said.

"I think these cyborgs are colder, more logical. They realize they have to fight to survive this," Magnus said. He wondered why more Terrans had not given up their natural bodies yet. He knew of a few that had, but it was not popular. He decided it was because, in VRs, they could already be anything they wanted to be—heroes, dragons, superstars. Artificial realities had become as important, if not more important, than real life in the Core Worlds decades ago.

"That's interesting. Could they have purposely submerged parts of their primitive brains?" Marcant wondered.

"That sounds like a good joint project for you and Maxsym to investigate... when things have calmed down," Telisa said.

Magnus felt the ship lift off. It was subtle. The new ship was superior in many ways to the first ships Magnus had served on. Shiny had accelerated progress in many technological areas that had previously leveled out.

Telisa expanded the team channel to include Maxsym over on the other ship.

"Maxsym. We've made progress over here. What's going on at your end?" she asked.

"All quiet on the Western Front," Maxsym said.

"What?"

"Sorry. An anachronism," he said.

"How do you know so much about the past?" she asked.

"I'm a student of history," Maxsym answered simply.

"I take it nothing unusual has happened," Magnus said, bringing the conversation back on point.

"Correct. No contact with the team. The only worrisome thing was that the battle sphere got rejected from the temple like our attendants. So they're on their own."

"We're coming to your position. We've made important contacts with another Celaran sect that can join us."

"So 'take me to your leader' actually works? Ah, nevermind that last," Maxsym said neutrally. He sounded distracted.

"Let's make sure it's still him," Magnus suggested to Telisa privately.

She held her hands out like asking 'how?'.

"Maxsym," Magnus began. "We made some observations of new Celaran behaviors while we were in that town."

"Really? Like what?"

"In low-calorie intake and high-stress conditions, the Celarans become violent," he said.

"Amazing! I'm not sure that makes any sense, though. Is it genetically triggered? Did Lee offer any insight?" Maxsym asked animatedly. His interest came through loud and clear to Magnus.

"Nothing yet," Magnus replied.

"That sounds like him," Magnus offered to Telisa privately.

"What now? How can we contact them?" Telisa asked on the channel.

"They're probably dead," Marcant said. "They had no chance against Trilisks, or even Trilisk machines that may have been left there."

Marcant's candor reminded Magnus a bit of Imanol. The difference was, though, that Imanol would have said it with the intention to provoke; Marcant was just being logical. He decided to respond with a like argument.

"Conjecture. It's too early to know that with any certainty," Magnus said. "We have to wait. Unless we can get creative and think of a workaround."

"I can tell when I'm being manipulated," Marcant said. "But Adair, Achaius, and I will think on it."

"Good," Magnus said.

Telisa looked at him and sighed. He could tell she was frustrated.

"Time to workout," Magnus said.

"You expect me to—"

"What better time? There's nothing we can do yet."

He knew she would reluctantly accept his advice. There was only one question left.

"Virtual or incarnate?"

"That was an easy mission—" Magnus started, then launched a punch directly at her face.

She dodged it easily.

Trilisk Special Forces.

"...so we should do some work incarnate," he finished.

Telisa nodded. They walked to the gym closest to their quarters on the assault ship. When they arrived, lights flicked on to show a wide open area with a relatively soft mat floor. The only hint of the many forms of exercise equipment the facility had were the barely visible seams in the mirrored wall where various apparatus would fold outward as needed.

"If every marine in the Space Force was like you..." he said.

"It doesn't matter much," she said. "Combat robots are still faster. They usually only miss me because they're programmed to fire at normal Terrans."

Of course, she was right. Even host bodies would not be more effective than frontline battle machines or Avatar battle modules like Cilreth had narrowly missed on Brighter Walken.

Unless they wield some alien toys. The breaker claws are amazingly good at taking out all kinds of robots.

They took off their Veer suits and squared off against each other in their undersheers. Magnus knew the drill. The workout would focus on him first.

He launched a series of attacks. Although his speed and coordination were excellent, she easily danced around his strikes and avoided his takedowns.

Sometimes, instead of dodging, she would stand and block. When Magnus kicked her forearm, she either blocked it hard or flipped his leg on by. When she blocked it, it felt like kicking a carbon support strut. When she hooked it, she added to his own force to throw him off balance. She mixed it up so that he did not know what to expect when.

Magnus shot for her legs. Telisa stopped him with a sharp hit on his shoulder, deflecting him. He rolled out of it and to the side. He ignored the frustration and kept trying. His normally well-coordinated moves became short and awkward when attempted on such a superior opponent.

They continued for twenty minutes, until Magnus staggered and slowed to a crawl. Then they took a break to drink and did two more ten-minute rounds. Magnus was unable to land a blow or achieve a lock.

"Let's switch," Magnus said, gasping for breath. He stepped toward the wall and one of the seams opened to allow him into a shower tube. He washed the sweat from his body for a few seconds. Then he emerged and put on his Veer skinsuit.

Telisa stood ready in her undersheers. Magnus allowed himself to drink in the sight for a moment. Still breathing heavily, he brought his hands back up.

"Your turn," he said.

Telisa went to work. She launched a side kick at his belly. The armored suit did its job; Magnus felt the impact across his entire torso rather than just the spot where her kick had landed. Even so, he grunted and fell back to the ground. He turned it into a roll, trying to come back up on guard.

Telisa was not in his field of vision. He felt two more blows fall across his back as she struck from behind. She concentrated on landing blows. They had found if she continually swept him to the ground, it ended up being more of a workout for him than for her.

Magnus lumbered around the workout area, taking hit after hit as a walking punching bag. He tried to anticipate and block whatever he could, but for the most part, it was a lost cause.

After half an hour, Telisa called a break through her link. Magnus dropped his arms and rested. She was barely breathing hard. When Telisa had first joined PIT, they had trained together and it was barely a workout for Magnus. Now the situation had reversed itself.

"Time to roll," she said. Another door opened in the mirrored wall and retrieved a thick garment. Magnus took off his Veer suit and did the same.

They grabbed each other by the collars and started. Here, too, they had developed their own set of rules to deal with Telisa's superior physical capabilities. Magnus tried to use strikes whenever he could to gain an advantage, while Telisa merely attempted to subdue him without harm.

Magnus launched an elbow at her face. When Telisa covered to absorb the blow, he trapped one of her arms and pulled it back with both of his, going for an armbar. Telisa let her arm extend and then tapped, even though they both knew he could not break it. She was too strong. Such concessions were necessary for Telisa to be a good training partner: Magnus had to be able to practice his techniques.

After another hour had passed, Magnus succumbed to the fatigue. His earthly muscles could only take so much. Telisa was fine; her enhanced musculature could replenish itself in real time and under load as long as she supplied the protein and calories necessary to fuel it.

Magnus stood up slowly and headed for the shower tube. He grunted. His body felt like it had been pummeled by a thousand rubber mallets.

"Workout's not over yet," she said from behind him. "You don't know your own limits. If we push it, you still have more in you."

Magnus turned to her and opened his mouth to reply to her slightly patronizing tone, but Telisa slipped her hands in under his drenched gi and opened it, letting the top fall to the ground. Her soft touch started to explore interesting places.

Oh.

"I... actually, I think maybe I can power through some more," he said.

"Good," she said, sweeping him once again.

***

Another day passed on the *Iridar*. Magnus knew that if the team did not show up soon, Telisa would start to talk about going in there herself. He contemplated the problem in his barren quarters. Magnus and Telisa had few personal possessions left after the crash of the last *Iridar*. They both kept weapons and armor littered in their sleeping spaces. The rest of their things were in a cargo bay workshop, where Telisa had artifacts and machines to study them and Magnus kept robot hardware. They did not even have to maintain their own fabricators anymore since Siobhan created everything they requested with astonishing efficiency.

Magnus leaned against his sleep web and sighed.

I'll need to convince her she can't go in there.

His mouth compressed. It was a tall order. Telisa would set her mind and then no one could stop her.

Is there any point in trying to win that one? No. Take a battle you can win and settle for convincing her to wait longer.

Soon, Telisa came to his quarters. She walked in without saying anything. Instead, she looked at him and waited for him to address the subject. He said nothing.

Telisa breached it anyway.

"They haven't returned yet. I may have to go in," Telisa said on the team channel.

"Ludicrous!" Marcant said before Magnus could say anything.

An unexpected ally. Good.

"No!" Magnus said with equal conviction.

"Think for a second. I'm a host body. Whatever defenses are set up may not activate against me."

Magnus made a quick adjustment to his argument. Marcant would be the logical one, so Magnus shifted to an emotional tack.

"I can't lose you," Magnus told her on a private channel.

"You're not going to lose me. Shiny will give you a replacement."

"Vaguely possible," Marcant was saying on the team channel. "But not worth risking your life on, especially when we have a team that walked in and hasn't come out yet," Marcant said. "Wait longer."

"A replacement would be very much like you. But a different person," Magnus said.

"This is how we've chosen to live. Dangerously, but with rich rewards," Telisa said to both of them.

"You're a hypocrite," Magnus said aloud. "You told us we were going to play it safe this time around."

"I'd be a hypocrite with a Trilisk AI in hand," Telisa said.

"Vines on fire! Calm down," Lee told them. "We have yet to see if the other team will come back."

Telisa laughed. "You think we're getting ahead of ourselves?" she said. "It's been too long."

"Wait another cycle of fresh starlight on the leaves," Lee said.

"You know, if everything is fine, and they're just not done yet as you suggest, then it won't hurt for me to go in there and join them," Telisa said.

"I didn't say everything is fine in there," Marcant said. "I suggested they're all dead."

"I was speaking more to Magnus and Lee's urging to wait longer," Telisa said.

"I also believe you should wait longer, or come up with another way to investigate the site," Maxsym chimed in. "If you go, you'll never hear my theory about why the Celarans become violent," he added.

Telisa stopped. She obviously wanted to go in, but she was not ready to ignore her entire team's input.

"Okay, I'll stay. Tell me," she said.

"Imagine you have twenty individuals going into a famine," Marcant said. "If everyone holds tight and weathers it out, maybe half of them survive. But those left are greatly weakened and left vulnerable to disease and predation."

"Ah. But if they fight, and some die..." Telisa continued.

"Yes. Then there are more resources left for the others. They would come out of the famine healthier, having divided the resources among fewer individuals from the beginning. The theory is somewhat akin to the way our bodies might drop muscle weight going into a famine in order to reduce caloric requirements."

"Seems logical. Which means it's probably wrong," Marcant said. "The truth is probably something weirder than we can imagine."

"What do you think, Telisa?" Maxsym asked.

"I think it was well worth staying for, Maxsym, thank you," Telisa said playfully.

Magnus remained worried.

We have another day at most before she goes in there anyway.

***

Magnus was remotely inching attendants around vines at the Trilisk site when his link received an urgent interrupt. It came from an attendant... one of the attendants from the team that had gone into the Trilisk temple.

"Telisa? Are you getting this? One of our attendants is asking for help from the outer system."

"It must have found something at last! Or do we have a new visitor?"

"Actually, neither," Marcant said. "This was Siobhan's attendant. I mean, the one of hers that was not kicked out of the temple!"

"What? How?" demanded Magnus.

"I don't even have a theory to put forward. It's happened before, but the attendants were always displaced on-planet."

"We sent attendants out there searching for enemy ships," Telisa said.

"This attendant is definitely not one of the ones we sent to scour the system. It says our team is being held prisoner on a Quarus ship! And... they request urgent extraction."

"Everyone get your gear! We're going in there," Telisa said.

"It could be a trick. It's *probably* a trick," Magnus said.

"Wait. You misunderstand," Marcant said. "They request extraction from the *new* location. Not the Trilisk complex under the temple."

"Out in space?" Telisa asked, exasperated.

"Apparently, yes," Marcant answered.

Could it be a distraction? For what purpose? Magnus asked himself.

Telisa changed tack quickly.

"Marcant! Get this ship en route now!" she ordered. "Maxsym. We may have found the other team. Get that ship ready for action!"

"Okay. Where are we going?"

"I sent you a pointer. Be ready for combat."

"Uhm, I'm hardly qualified—"

"That Vovokan ship will run itself in a fight," Telisa interrupted him. "Do you know how to tell it to fight for you?"

"Yes," Maxsym said, though his voice cracked.

"Good. Here's our course," Telisa said.

Under Marcant's direction, the Terran assault ship lifted off from Celara Palnod.

Michael McCloskey

Chapter 15

Siobhan blinked. Dark gray walls surrounded her.

"Where is it?!" she barked. She spastically turned her weapon left then right, searching for the Trilisk machine.

After another moment, she saw that the uneven gray tones were not on the surfaces around her: they were shifting shadows beyond translucent walls. She was trapped in an empty transparent box only of perhaps ten meters on a side.

It's not here!

She stood and listened. Nothing.

No, it's that I'm not there.

"Telisa? Team?" Her team channel was empty.

Her eyes adjusted to the dim light. She saw dark shapes through the walls... banks of alien machines in all directions. There were no portals in the clear walls, the floor, or the ceiling.

Her stealth sphere had deactivated. It responded to her status request, telling her it was ready to cloak her on command. She was alone and visible.

"Where am I?" she asked aloud as if pleading for someone to hear her.

Siobhan reached forward and placed a hand against the wall. It was cool and smooth. She peered through the fog outside but then realized it was not fog.

That's water! Or some liquid. An alien environment...

She spoke her conclusion aloud.

"Quarus! Frackedpackets!"

That explained why the machines around her now looked so different. Trilisk constructs almost always had smooth and simple exteriors. Each bank of machinery she saw through the dim water had an accompanying host of tubes and complex surface features. What light there was came from long glow strips on the ceiling outside her prison.

Movement caught her eye. A dark form approached her chamber from the outside. Siobhan immediately flipped over into stealth mode.

Something bumped against the clear chamber that trapped her. Siobhan recoiled from the clear wall she had touched.

"Calm down... calm down," she said in half-panic.

Siobhan heard a loud snap, causing her to jump again.

"Five Holies!" said a familiar voice.

Siobhan turned to see Telisa9 right beside her.

"Where? What?" Siobhan asked. Telisa9 did not respond. Siobhan realized her stealth sphere had dampened the sound.

"Stealth yourself!" Siobhan sent over her link. Telisa9 turned into an echoform overlaid onto Siobhan's vision.

"What happened?" Siobhan asked.

"That Trilisk machine got me. I thought I was dead," Telisa9 said. "Where are we now?"

"It's a reverse aquarium. We're on the inside," Siobhan summarized.

"How could we possibly... end up in a Quarus cage?"

Siobhan had no answer.

The dark shape Siobhan had caught sight of earlier neared one of the clear walls. It resolved into a black robot. It had the streamlined shape of a huge fish, much taller than its girth. There were no eyes or mouth, however, where the mouth of a fish might be, a sharp spike extended to tap against the clear wall.

Even though it seemed futile, Telisa9 and Siobhan both leveled their weapons at the thing. A whining noise started up. A small white spot formed on the clear wall where the thing had contacted it.

"It's cutting in here!" Siobhan announced.

"Why would it do that? We're trapped."

"I don't know, but it must know we're here. Our stealth spheres were both off when we arrived."

"Prepare your suit for immersion," Telisa9 ordered.

"My suit only has a half hour of life support available," Siobhan said. "That's mostly water out there, right? We need some kind of electrolysis unit."

"Our problems are much more immediate," Telisa9 said. "First off, if that thing makes a hole the outside pressure is coming in here. We could be crushed. Secondly, if we survive that, I suspect that robot is not nice."

A sharp snap announced Caden's arrival in the cage. One attendant had arrived with him; it immediately started to orbit him.

"Welcome to the party," Telisa9 said dryly over their link connection.

"Stealth yourself!" Siobhan snapped.

His eyes widened.

"Siobhan? You're alive! We're alive!"

Siobhan smiled to see him, even in such dire circumstances. "Maybe not for long."

Caden saw the danger quickly.

"What's that thing?" he asked. He faded from sight to be replaced by his echoform.

"Which one do you mean? The Quarus robot drilling in here?"

"We don't *know* that's a Quarus machine," Telisa9 corrected.

"Why did it put us in here just to cut us out? This is crazy," Caden said. He sounded more stressed than Siobhan had ever heard him.

"The Trilisk machine did this," Telisa9 said. "Not the Quarus, I think."

Siobhan tried to remain calm and think about that for a moment.

That Trilisk thing could probably have killed us. But it sent us here... to die?

Another shadowy form materialized from the murk behind the robot. It was a monstrous looking thing with four long, chitinous legs. The legs intersected at a softer-looking round mass, waving with tentacles. Siobhan blinked. Her mind tried to resolve the shape as a giant octopus eating a spider crab, but it did not quite work.

"Is that a Quarus?" she asked.

At first, the others could not tell what she referred to, but they found it quickly.

"Ugh! Purple paste!" Caden commented in disgust.

"Is that one organism?" Telisa9 asked.

"The legs look like crab legs," Caden said. "The rest? Ugh! It's going to cut in here and kill us! I say we open fire now," Caden said.

"Yes. What choice do we have?" Siobhan agreed.

"Calm down!" Telisa9 ordered. "I want non-suicidal ideas, people."

Arakaki appeared beside her with a loud snap.

"What—"

"We're trapped in a cage, and a robot is drilling in here to get us," Siobhan summarized.

Arakaki activated her stealth sphere. "Let it weaken the wall for us," she said. "It's not getting *in*. We're getting *out*."

"We'll be easy targets once this fills with water," Caden said.

Arakaki took a second to digest the situation.

"We all have suits, and we have at least half an hour of oxygen," Arakaki replied. Her echoform tossed her projectile weapon aside and drew a laser pistol.

"I don't think that laser is going to work with bubbles in the water," Caden said.

"Well, it'll be better than the submachine gun," Arakaki said. "Besides, there are no bubbles yet."

"Keep them both," Telisa9 said. "We might find a way up and out of here."

Arakaki shrugged and retrieved her carbine from the floor.

Up out of here? It's a long shot, but worth a try.

"The ceiling," Siobhan said. "I say we blow a hole through it while we still have air."

"There'll be water on the other side!" Caden protested.

"Gravity is pulling us this way," Siobhan pointed out. "The best way to escape liquid is to ascend out of it."

"Why is the ceiling curved like that?" Arakaki asked.

"It *does* curve. Are we in space or under an ocean?" Caden asked.

"Too many unknowns," Arakaki said. "We could be in a submarine under the surface."

"The ceiling might curve for added strength against huge pressures," Telisa9 said.

"The gravity here is stronger," Siobhan realized.

"Are you sure?" Caden asked.

"Yes. It's strong," Siobhan said. "We aren't on Celara Palnod anymore."

Abruptly a spray of water erupted from the cell wall where the alien machine had been working.

"Time's up!" Arakaki said.

Telisa9 pointed to the ceiling. "Do it!"

"Protect your heads, this may ricochet," Arakaki said. She pointed her carbine upward and at an angle that would direct projectile bounces into the far corner of the chamber. Then she covered her face with her other armored arm.

Siobhan told her suit to extend its helmet and looked away with an arm over her face.

Ratatatat! Ratatatat!

A hissing noise followed the immensely loud gunfire. Siobhan's ears popped. Her suit's soft faceplate flipped down and hardened into a visor. At the same time, she felt the suits' gloves deploy over her hands. She clenched her new hand. She could feel the glove on it, but the sensation did not feel normal yet.

"Okay, that was *not* expected," Arakaki said.

Siobhan looked up. The weapon had punched holes in the ceiling. Instead of water coming in, their air had blown out.

Siobhan looked back to the wall of the cage. The machine was drilling another hole. The pressure of the water coming through the first opening was strong, but not as bad as Siobhan had feared. Also, the clear material that had been breached did not give any signs of nearing catastrophic failure.

"The water isn't spraying in *that* hard," Arakaki said. "We aren't at the bottom of an ocean. Probably a shallow body of water or a spacecraft."

It has to weaken that panel some more. We have a little more time!

Telisa9 tried a laser on the ceiling. It cut through, so she connected the holes so that a piece the size of a large dinner tray fell down into the cage.

"It's a double bulkhead," she said, shining her weapon's light into the hole. "There wasn't any water inside!"

"So if we cut through the next one, will it fill with water or eject us into space?" Caden asked. Siobhan heard the desperation in his voice and felt the same in herself.

"Into space," Telisa9 answered. "Our last attendant just verified that there's vacuum beyond this second bulkhead."

Fight in water or be ejected into space? How did we get into such a terrible position?

"That space up there was not pressurized. We haven't lost all the air, but we lowered the pressure considerably," Telisa9 said.

"Making it easier for that thing to break in," Caden said. Siobhan supposed he might be right. The pressure on their side had been reduced.

Two streams of water flowed into the cage now. The machine drilled at the third corner of about a square meter.

"The water will flood this part," Telisa9 said calmly. "We should crawl up there. It's cover, and we can fight."

But we'd be trapped up there.

"If they damage the other bulkhead, we'll be blown into space," Caden pointed out.

"You'd rather stay here and fight those things *underwater*?" Arakaki snapped. She threw a smart rope into the hole. The rope slid itself upward into the space they had discovered, forming a ring around the far side of the ragged hole to anchor itself.

The team scrabbled up into the space between the bulkheads in record time. More water sprayed in below them.

"I could use the rest of the power in this laser to boil a bunch of water. Even though it wouldn't be air, just water vapor, it might increase the pressure enough to keep this space from flooding?" Arakaki suggested.

This is hopeless. We need to make a game-changing move, not hide here and die. Siobhan spotted their last remaining attendant and had an idea.

"No. Punch a hole in the next bulkhead," she said.

"What?" everyone else said simultaneously.

"Get me a hole big enough to get this attendant out. It can operate in space and send a message. Let the rest of the team know we're in trouble!"

Big trouble.

"What? Into the vacuum of space that's beyond this?" Caden asked.

"Screw ourselves to let it out?" Arakaki asked, joining Caden in protest.

137

"Yes. We let it out and send a message for help. Does it look like we're getting out of here by ourselves?"

As she spoke, a section of the clear material below gave way. Huge amounts of water poured into the chamber where they had been trapped.

Telisa9 looked thoughtful. "Punching a hole in the outer bulkhead could be catastrophic."

"A ship this advanced will have patching protocols in place. Most likely it will repair itself within a few seconds," Siobhan asserted.

"It might repair it by filling this entire bulkhead space with quick drying foam," Caden said.

"We're desperate. I say we get word out," Siobhan said. The water level had almost filled the chamber below, and it was still rising.

Arakaki shrugged. "Okay. I'm in."

"Do it," Telisa9 said.

Arakaki shot a projectile into the outer bulkhead. The round shattered. Siobhan felt her Veer suit absorb a ricochet.

"This one's much stronger."

"Grenade," Telisa9 instructed. "Tell it to direct the energy toward the bulkhead, focused to a little larger than an attendant-sized area."

Arakaki took out a grenade and told it to attach to the ceiling as water started to fill their chamber. She motioned toward the other side of the space.

"Get some space," she said. "As long as the grenade's not in the water, I hope the shock wave won't be too much."

Everyone dropped to the floor. Churning water continued to come in through the hole they had created. The air pressure rose to resist it, slowing the flow. Siobhan grimly realized that if they were indeed in space, blowing a hole in the ceiling would break the equilibrium and they would lose what air they had left. If enough pressure was lost, the water would boil away, too.

What other choice do we have? They were alone on an alien ship and it was filled with *water*, not air.

Siobhan had time to glance below as the water covered her faceplate. She saw the thin robot smashing through a plate of the cage and struggling to enter the chamber below. She glanced at her new hand, even though she could not see it directly with her Veer suit's gloves extended.

Of all the times to have a new hand... I don't need any more problems!

Ka-Wump!

The blast still caused a shockwave she could feel, even with the grenade programmed to hit the hull with everything it had. The outer shell of the grenade blasted away and struck the water. Suddenly Siobhan could barely see anything. The room filled with swirling water and bubbles.

Here we go.... vacuum!

Her heart pounded in her chest as a new release of adrenaline poured through her blood.

Even for me, this is crazy...

"I sent the attendant through!" Caden told them.

The water continued to boil away. Siobhan assumed that they had created a hole into space which was sucking away their air and the water vapor. A hand grabbed her wrist.

"Hold on here!" Caden told her.

She felt the edge of the hole they had created to get through the inner bulkhead. She grabbed it and held on. She could feel water moving into the chamber, causing her body to shift about.

Siobhan was not sure if it had been five seconds or fifty, but finally, the chamber calmed. She did not look up to catch a glimpse of how the hole might have been patched; she was concerned about the things *below* them.

"They're right below us now," Siobhan warned. She felt completely unable to defend herself.

Their space was now almost full of water after the boil-off and the new seal.

The ship is compensating as we predicted. It makes sense, they must be able to maintain the environment within their norms, as long as the damage is not too severe.

"Argh!" Arakaki erupted.

"What is it?" Caden asked.

Hisssss.

Arakaki fired her laser downward. Then she swam to one side as bubbles rose from below.

"It's that robot," she said. "It burned me. I don't see the alien."

Siobhan could not tell how bad Arakaki had been hurt through the cloaking. Her echoform appeared intact, but Siobhan did not know how accurate that was.

"It probably fled when we breached the outer hull," Telisa9 said. Siobhan saw Telisa9 held her breaker claw.

"Don't!" Siobhan urged. "If it explodes nearby in the water, we'll be crushed by the shock wave."

Underwater pressure waves were especially dangerous for creatures with air-filled lungs, even when they wore Veer suits. The explosive grenades would be dangerous. The same went for their breaker claws, which often caused explosions when part of their targets' power rings became insulative.

"My laser didn't stop it!" Arakaki said.

"Take turns, clockwise from me, hit it with your lasers," Telisa9 said, pointing her laser pistol at the opening. She fired.

Caden was next. His rifle was harder to line up, so he stood and shot downward. Siobhan could barely see evidence of the shots in the water, but tiny particles must have been absorbing the energy and burning, causing a slight glow in the initial path.

"I got a kill confirmation," Caden said. Siobhan felt a huge relief. It had died easier than she thought it might.

"Everyone down there. We need to rally and hit them before they feel safe again," Telisa9 said. "Siobhan, find oxygen or a power source."

Siobhan thought Telisa9's idea was sound. The hole in the hull would have caused the aliens below to scramble to secure themselves. Once they realized the breach had been fixed, they would come back.

The adrenaline flowed through her system. It usually made her feel better than this. Being trapped on a Quarus ship was not a flavor of excitement she enjoyed.

At least it's warm, she thought. *But not too warm.*

She wondered what would have happened if the water had been above Terran body temperature. The suits would only have been able to keep them cool for so long without any way to evaporate moisture.

"It could be worse," she told Caden privately.

"We'll make it," he said.

She smiled. She was usually the one telling him some crazy thing would work.

Arakaki led the way. She swam through the hole back into their 'cage' followed by Telisa9. Caden swam through next. Siobhan paused to look at the ceiling. Only a slender pocket of air or water vapor remained at the top of the little chamber. It did not look like enough for even one breath. She swam down through the hole after her teammates.

"If there were any real troops in here I think we'd already be dead," Arakaki transmitted. She held a laser in one hand and a long blade in her other. Siobhan assumed it was one of the amazingly sharp blades that were dangerous to carry.

Our lasers barely work, we're afraid to use breaker claws... grim. She supposed an elite soldier in her position would make a joke about alien sushi with great elan.

Siobhan's link received a notification that Arakaki fired her laser. Siobhan saw a flash in the water. Siobhan did not know what she could do to help, so she turned to cover the flank. She immediately saw a torpedo-shaped machine with four mechanical arms pulling away a section of the cage.

"Robot over here," Siobhan snapped.

"Take it out," Telisa9 said. "No breakers."

Siobhan did not want to use the laser. She knew that energy could provide oxygen. Instead, she manually selected her PAW's projectile weapon and configured it for underwater. In a second the weapon told her it had adjusted the settings, but did not have the correct type of ammunition for submarine use.

"Cut that leg off!" Caden called out. Siobhan assumed he was talking about another fight.

Siobhan pushed off straight for the robot, bringing her to point blank range and fired anyway.

Thump, thump, thump.

Bubbles erupted outward from her weapon, accompanied by vibrations she could feel through her suit. The robot was obscured. The rounds did not report any hits.

No way I missed! It's got to be that those rounds don't work right underwater.

The bubbles cleared away, revealing that the machine had been torn open. It sank in two pieces, arms still. She smiled.

Knew it.

Siobhan swept for enemies again and did not see any. She turned and swam toward the others. She saw Arakaki riding a long crab-arm with her blade out. She sliced through the limb, detaching it and dropping her back to the floor. Bright red blood poured through the water.

Siobhan tried to assess the damage to the alien.

"Are you winning?" she asked urgently.

"It's hard to kill," Caden said. He placed the end of his combo rifle against the mass at the center and fired.

Thump, thump.

More blood and bubbles exploded through the water.

"Hold your fire. I think it's dead," Telisa9 said.

"It's still moving!"

"I think it's... I think that's how it dies."

Siobhan noted the Quarus had many tears in its flesh. Two of its huge legs had been carved off. It still moved, but not in any coordinated fashion. Ugly short tentacles waved around its body.

"We need to find oxygen or start producing it," Telisa9 said.

"That drained our cells even further," Arakaki noted grimly.

"We can use the cell in my stun baton," Siobhan offered.

"Caden, find materials we can use to separate and collect oxygen. Siobhan, see if you can detect any free oxygen around here. For all we know, there's a tank full of it in this room."

Caden started to search. "These machines are so blocky. I don't think they're filled with water. I think the spaces inside are mostly solid," Caden said.

"Well, if they were hollow, then any electrical connections would short," Siobhan said.

"Theories," Telisa9 said.

Siobhan half walked, half swam around their cage, scanning. Caden ripped a clear hemisphere of glass or plastic off one of the machines. Siobhan assumed it was to collect gases.

Siobhan neared the Quarus corpse. She saw a part of it wriggle again.

Damn that thing is creepy. The fact it won't stop moving is—

Her device told her it got a hit nearby.

"My sensor has found free oxygen!" Siobhan reported.

"What? Where?" Telisa9 gasped.

"Here. Inside that corpse."

"By the Five. In the alien's body?"

"That makes sense. These things live in water. They're probably carbon-based, so their metabolism uses oxygen, like ours," Arakaki said.

And their blood is red like ours, so uses an iron-based carrier.

"So it has oxygen in it. So what? The water does, too. We would have to separate it," Caden said.

"No, I said free oxygen!" Siobhan said. "There's a hollow space inside that thing. Some kind of gas bladder with almost pure oxygen in it."

Arakaki swam forward.

"Point if you can. I don't want to cut the organ open," she said.

"If you uncloak, I can send you this feed and you can overlay it," Siobhan replied. She uncloaked and Arakaki followed suit.

Siobhan sent the feed from her device to Arakaki's link. After a moment, Arakaki took her blade and started to cut.

More of the blood came pouring out. Siobhan was struck again by how much it resembled Terran blood. Arakaki looked like a mad diver cutting into a giant octopus, except the blood was red, not blue.

"It's still moving," Arakaki noted.

"Yes," Siobhan agreed nervously.

"Cover me," Arakaki said.

"You got it," Caden said, heading over.

"No, get ready to start electrolysis," Telisa9 ordered. Her echoform moved over toward Arakaki and the growing garden of blood swirling around her.

New threads of red fluid intermingled with the water as she cut.

"Red blood like us?" Telisa9 commented.

"Maxsym would say: I wonder if they use the same oxygen transport molecule. I say, get the oxygen and leave it."

"Actually, someone take a sample of its blood or its flesh," Telisa9 ordered. "If we get out of this alive, Maxsym will owe us big time."

An ugly purple organ sac floated upward, trailing connective tissue. It was as large as Arakaki's torso. Arakaki handled it carefully. She left the last bit of flesh connected to keep the sac from dragging her to the ceiling.

"It's in that," she said.

Arakaki cut it carefully. Some bubbles escaped from a tube, so she pinched it shut.

"Siobhan. Carefully, take this weapon. I don't have enough hands for this."

Siobhan pushed herself forward through the water and took the ultrasharp. Arakaki pulled out a suit hose from her shoulder.

"I'm going to try and extract it all. We can't hand this mess back and forth without losing a lot of the contents. Once I have it, we'll transfer it between our suits which will have a much better seal."

Arakaki punched the nozzle of her suit hose into the soft tube that had leaked before. The sac visibly deflated. The entire area had an even red haze now that the blood had dispersed. Siobhan wondered how quickly the ship would filter it out.

"Got it."

It sent its robot in here to kill us. Now it has saved us. Or at least, bought us time to die another way.

Arakaki discarded the organ and connected to Siobhan's suit.

"It won't go as far four ways, but here you are," she said.

Siobhan's suit reported the replenishment of oxygen. It did not have enough storage for all of it in its pressurized cannister, so she configured the suit to release nitrogen and increase the oxygen content within the suit. Arakaki distributed the rest of the oxygen.

Siobhan breathed deeply. Every breath felt like pure life. She had been in some close calls with low oxygen supplies before, but not while trapped in a liquid-filled alien ship. She handed the blade back to Arakaki.

"How long do we have?" Telisa9 asked.

"That added forty more minutes. I'm showing almost an hour of survivability. We have to get out of here soon," Caden said, stating the obvious.

"Or find another one to kill," Arakaki said.

Okay, she's scary.

"Set up to get oxygen from the water," Telisa9 ordered.

"We don't have a PEM block," Siobhan said. "There are several back on the *Iridar*."

"Not membrane electrolysis, I mean the primitive way. It takes power, but our lasers aren't useful if we're already dead."

"Maybe we can find a power ring around here and figure out how to bleed off some of its field," Caden suggested.

"Then get looking. In the meantime, assume we're using the stun baton's cell. Arakaki, keep watch. Tell us if more are coming," Telisa9 ordered.

Siobhan pushed her tall frame through the water. It resisted her efforts, dragging each limb on every movement. Her low-gravity origins had found yet another way to punish her.

You wanted danger. You got it, she told herself, breathing rapidly.

Michael McCloskey

Chapter 16

Magnus watched the tactical as the two PIT ships hurtled out toward the SOS they had received. He still wondered if the transmission had been a decoy meant to draw them away from the planet, but with so little information, it made sense to respond as if the message were genuine.

"There's nothing out there," Maxsym said from the Vovokan *Iridar*. His tense voice gave away his state of mind.

"Let me help you with our sensors," Magnus said. "If there's some way to coordinate our search, we could split the area, but I don't know how to share the search patterns between a Terran ship and a Vovokan one." He looked at Telisa next to him in the bridge-lounge of the Terran *Iridar*, imploring her to join.

"I'll help too," she said. "All three of us might be as good as one Cilreth."

"I thought her specialty was Vovokan software," Maxsym said.

"Her specialty was finding people," Telisa said. "But she was good at everything related to coordinating missions from back on the ship."

Her way of trying to avoid the danger. Although she was brave so many times. Maybe she was more afraid of letting us down in a combat situation.

"How about we search spinward from the reported location and Maxsym takes the other side?" Telisa suggested.

Magnus opened up an ECCM suite in his PV. He found a saved configuration for detecting cloaked Celaran ships and tried it out.

His new pane came up. It did not detect any anomalies at the source of the transmission. He started a scan pattern for a hemispherical volume spinward of the reported target, then tried to think of another approach.

"It's possible our Terran scanners aren't up to this," Magnus said.

"I can help," Marcant said. "Maxsym, you'll be receiving my request to use your ship's sensors from here, if you can authorize me—"

"Yes, yes, that much I can do," Maxsym said.

Telisa and Magnus waited for a minute while Marcant searched using the Vovokan ship's superior technology.

"There's something there! A cloaked ship," Marcant told them. "We never would have noticed it without the attendant call."

"Vovokan? Celaran?"

"I don't think so," Marcant said. "I don't know."

Marcant doesn't say that very often.

"No reason to think it's not Quarus as the message said. The Quarus must have taken a page from the Celarans," Magnus said. "We know they've learned to detect cloaked Celarans, so..."

"So they've probably learned cloaking tricks of their own," Telisa finished.

"How can we land on this vine?" Lee asked.

Telisa's mouth was set. She was thinking furiously.

She's not going to give up on them, that's for sure. The only question is how to go about saving them.

"It may not matter. I see other ships out here," Maxsym said. "We have to get out of the system now!"

"What?" Telisa said. "We don't see them."

"One moment..."

A dozen more ships appeared on the *Iridar's* tactical.

"A whole fleet? Maybe we do have to run," Magnus said.

"Those are Celaran ships!" Marcant interjected.

Most of the contacts in Magnus's PV changed color to green. The remainder were still changing to green one at a time. The original one remained red.

"How did we miss them before?" Telisa demanded.

"I don't think they were *there* before," Maxsym said.

"Contact them," Telisa said. "Can we do that without giving ourselves away?"

"It certainly raises the danger. But we're all at long range right now," Marcant said.

"Then we have to. Get one of them on the channel!"

"I'll try. But if these are Celarans from some other faction, they won't be able to understand us anytime soon," Marcant said.

A few more seconds ticked by. Magnus saw another entity joined the channel, but its identification headers were non-standard.

"You have it," Marcant said.

"We've discovered a hidden Quarus ship in the system," Telisa transmitted.

"Trunk of a huge vine, that's a space station. We believe it was left to monitor the fate of our homeworld," came the reply. The Terran communication protocols finally resolved the speaker as Cynan.

"Is that really you, Cynan?" Telisa asked.

"Yes."

"Your friends knew about the Quarus station?"

"Watch the threat underleaf, we have been preparing to strike back against them."

Now he speaks as if he's been one of the Cylerans all along. He has been, I suppose, just separated from them.

"Our friends went into a Trilisk compound on Celara Palnod, now one of their attendants has shown up at this location!" Magnus said. "It carried a message saying that they're in trouble, trapped inside that station."

"Could the Quarus have faked the message?" Cynan asked.

"That's what I'm wondering. How is it our team is there at all? Maybe this is a trick," Magnus said.

"It would be very difficult for them to fake. The Vovokan protocols are secure," Marcant said on the shared channel. "Especially given the Quarus' extremely alien methods of communicating in large batches of information."

"Then how?"

"Could the Quarus be working with the Trilisks?" asked Marcant.

If that's true, then we're outmatched. Just when it looked like the Space Force and the Celarans had a chance.

"I don't know," Telisa said. "But if there are Trilisks involved, it's probably that one of the Quarus leaders here might be a Trilisk. It could be like the situation back on Earth before the revolution."

Magnus nodded.

"Cynan? We need to help our people right away. They could be running out of breathable air," Telisa said.

"The star is bright overhead, our schedule can be accelerated," said Cynan.

"We have to go in now. Half our team is over there," Telisa said.

"Vines on fire, I'll see if I can convince my comrades to join you."

"Thank you," Telisa said.

"What can we do when we get there?" Maxsym said.

"If our team has been captured, we can't open fire on the ship," Marcant said.

"This is a commando vessel," Magnus reminded them. "Though its main focus is drop attacks, it's also equipped for ship-to-ship incursion. We'll have to board them."

"Equipped how?" asked Maxsym.

"We have remoras for knocking out ship electronics, as well as a spinner auto-matcher to delay the Pirate's

Option. The port and starboard hatches are designed for breaching target hatches, or even enemy ship hulls in some cases," Magnus said.

"Slow down there!" Maxsym said. "That ship might be much more powerful than ours. We don't even know how large it is or if there's more than one. We could be outmatched. Even if you manage to disable it for a while, how can you board an alien ship filled with water?"

Filled with water. Damn, I hadn't even thought of that.

"I have to say I agree with Maxsym here," Marcant said. "Our ships are small and there are only a few of us. We aren't equipped to assault a ship with a liquid atmosphere. We haven't trained for something like that."

"We have the battle spheres," Telisa pointed out.

"They can be effective even in water," Achaius said on the channel.

"Perhaps too effective," Adair said. "We would have to worry about blowing entire parts of that ship away, including those containing the team."

Magnus listened to the AIs carefully. They did not seem to agree with each other.

Is this what it's like in Marcant's personal channel? He has those two AIs chattering at him all the time?

The minutes ticked by while the two ships used their gravity spinners at full power to accelerate. Though their drives were able to translate out of FTL quickly, the gravity drive could not quickly bring them beyond light speed, especially not mid-system. It would take over an hour to arrive at the location of the stealthed base.

"Our forces will join you on the vine," Cynan said. "We wish to repay you for your assistance at our colony."

"That's fantastic. Marcant, can you—"

"Coordinating our intercept courses on the target base," Marcant said.

"We might actually have a chance of getting them out alive now," Telisa said to Magnus privately.

"I suggest we head to the arsenal," Magnus said, rising to his feet. She got up to follow him. Magnus felt admiration.

There's no questioning whether or not we're going in, even into a ship filled with water. Those are our people out there.

"I hate to mention this..." Magnus said.

"Marcant, please inform the Cylerans of my... condition," Telisa asked publicly. "If I'm taken by a Trilisk, they should be able to take me out."

"Maybe you shouldn't go in at all," Marcant said.

"The Trilisks are almost all gone. There's not one hiding under every rock. I'm going in to get our people."

They walked in silence for a moment.

"I suppose we should go in with only one ship?" Telisa asked, changing the subject. "Having three spinners there so close together must be even more dangerous?"

"Actually, no. Bringing in two spinners under our control is to our advantage as long as we coordinate perfectly. It gives us more power to control the gravitational eddies that would result from intentional mismatch," Marcant answered.

"Then I leave it to you to coordinate with their assault ship," she said.

They took a left turn and came to the door of the armory. The door opened for their links and they went in to see what they had.

"They want to spread the weight across two vines by putting some of their cyborgs on this ship for the attack," Lee said on the team channel.

Apparently she is in separate contact with Cynan.

"That's welcome," Telisa said. "We only have the battle spheres, Magnus, and me."

"Seriously? You're going in there?" Marcant asked.

"We'll let the machines go first," Telisa said as if that explained it all. "We need to arrange a mid-trip rendezvous," Telisa said.

"I'm working with them now," Marcant said.

"Maxsym, keep your distance with your ship. Stay vigilant and let us know if any other ships approach. When this one gets attacked, they may call for any local reinforcements that might still be hiding around the system."

"Will do," he replied.

"If things get dicey and you're not sure you're going to make it, sacrifice an attendant and send word back to the Space Force," Magnus said.

"Very well," Maxsym said dourly.

He doesn't like the idea of dying out here. Can't say I blame him.

"What do we have that works in water? The lasers, the breaker claws, and... ?" he pondered aloud.

"Well, at least some of the water will be draining," she said. "Don't rule out projectiles completely. Here, we have one box of water rounds." Her eyes swept over the arsenal. "Lasers, grenades, and breakers. We have these ultrasharp swords, but... no range and I imagine it's hard to swing one underwater."

Magnus nodded. He set down his rifle, which he felt would be too unwieldy underwater. He replaced it with a laser pistol, two extra energy rings, and another grenade. Then he loaded another pistol with the water rounds and added it to his belt.

"What does a stunner do underwater?" Telisa asked.

Magnus considered it. On the one hand, water transmitted the vibrations better over distance, but on the other hand, it would presumably take a lot more energy to shake water than air. Also, he wondered if the directionality of the stunner would be affected.

"Probably makes an awful noise, but I doubt it would work. Well, against Terrans. Who knows what it would do to Quarus? They could be sensitive."

Telisa left the stunners on the rack. "I don't know if they're even waterproof."

"I'm afraid the Quarus will school us on what's effective underwater," Magnus said.

"We need to research better weapons for underwater use," Telisa said.

"The Space Force has some," Magnus said. "We can look into it for later, but we don't have time to fabricate any. This is what we've got. The breakers and grenades will work well as long as we make sure we're not where the shock wave will get us, too."

"Even if we're somehow not in the water, we might kill our teammates that way," Telisa pointed out.

"We have a solution for rendezvous in ten minutes," Marcant said. "They can enter through vacuum, so I'll house them in the assault bays and drop them off the same way."

Magnus and Telisa traded looks.

"I guess we won't be going into an airlock," Magnus said.

"Waterlock," Telisa corrected. "Yeah I guess not. This could get messy."

"So you're imagining the same thing I am: we're going to enter through holes boiling water off into space, while who knows what is shooting at us."

Telisa grabbed a combo laser-projectile PAW and loaded it with water rounds. She took some grenades and they headed for the assault bays on the belly of the ship. Within a couple of minutes, they arrived at a lock door and paused. Vibrations ran through the deck.

"We're opening the doors," Marcant said.

Magnus waited. He felt uncomfortable, but could not quite figure out why for a moment.

"I know you feel the need to help our team, but maybe we should stand this one out," Magnus said.

"Why?" Telisa asked. "It's not like you to get cold feet."

"Those Cyleran battle machines must each be worth a hundred of me, and at least ten of you as a host body. The same goes for the Vovokan battle spheres. I'm not sure we're going to do anything except make targets of ourselves out there."

"Well I wasn't planning on leading the charge. Even the Space Force follows up the machines with the marines, right? Machines are first-in, first-out."

"There's also the Pirate's Option," Magnus reminded her. "This base may be going out with a bang. We could be stuck."

"I hear you. I wouldn't be doing this if we didn't have team members over there. We have to get them back."

Magnus nodded. At least if he died, he figured Shiny had plenty of copies of him out there somewhere.

"We have the Cyleran assault machines aboard," Marcant said. "They're waiting with the Vovokan battle spheres."

Magnus checked the lock with his link. The bay had pressurized on the other side. They walked through together.

Massive Cylerans waited in a clean white room 50 meters across. Each of the alien cyborgs was the size of a Terran land vehicle. Magnus spotted the Vovokan battle machines in the back.

"Thank you all for helping us save our trapped friends," Telisa transmitted.

Magnus was about to say that Cynan may not have equipped them with Terran link protocols when one answered.

"It is us who welcome your assistance protecting the vine. The Screamers must be stopped."

The assault bay offered Telisa and Magnus space exoskeletons. Magnus accepted the service through his link. A white panel opened from the wall behind them.

"What's this? For space operations?" Telisa asked.

"Yes. We want these. It'll be better than relying on our attendants to shuttle us around," Magnus said.

A pair of exoskeletons walked out of the panel. The frames quickly adjusted size to fit each of them. Magnus had used the exoskeletons before; they were designed for space infantry, basically powered frames with rocket assist capability that would allow them to maneuver in space.

Magnus accessed the tactical and watched the assault develop in his PV. He saw the PIT ships and seven Cyleran vessels approaching the stealthed Quarus base. Six of the Celaran vessels continued to accelerate. Their projected courses were on the tactical.

"It looks like those Celaran ships are maneuvering for an attack pass," Magnus said.

"It makes sense. They'll draw fire away from us and mix it up. Give us a chance to come in and attack at point blank range."

Magnus knew they took a huge risk. If the remoras failed to disable the Quarus ship, they would likely all be blown to bits by the base's main weaponry. Magnus watched as the squadron of Cyleran ships started their run-by within weapons range, trying to draw fire from the Quarus base.

The combat control summary from the bridge showed the *Iridar* had launched a spread of remoras to disable the target. A group of missiles launched from nearby Cyleran ships at the same time, mirroring their trajectory.

"We don't want to destroy the base!" Magnus sent on the team channel.

"Diversions only, I'm assured," Marcant said. "There's a type of disabler missile of their own mixed in among that salvo, similar to our own remoras only more sophisticated."

Telisa and Magnus shuffled in place nervously as the battle unfolded. The Cyleran soldiers stoically remained motionless and silent. One of the Cyleran ships blossomed into a ball of energy, struck down by weapons unknown. Many of the Cyleran missiles also blinked out, presumably destroyed by Quarus point defenses. The remoras reached their target along with the remaining missiles and disappeared from the tactical.

The *Iridar* crept closer and closer, slowing to meet the enemy.

"I think they're disabled or else we would already be hit. Identify any external weapons and take them out now," Telisa said.

Magnus remained silent, jaw clenched.

Here we go. Just another day on the PIT team.

The tactical had zoomed in as the *Iridar* approached, showing Magnus the appropriate level of detail. Now the tactical stopped changing its boundaries, which meant that they had come into position and stopped relative to the target. A second later, the bay lights went out and the assault bay doors opened. The Cyleran machines shot out into space within another second. The Vovokan spheres followed quickly, leaving Telisa and Magnus.

"The heavies are out," Telisa said. "We'll join them within the minute."

Marcant sent back a nonverbal acknowledgment. Telisa activated her exoskeleton thrusters and headed slowly for the lock. Magnus stayed on her right.

Magnus saw flashes in the darkness. The Cylerans and their assault ship traded shots with Quarus defenses. Nothing came their way for a second, then the *Iridar* started to fire into the base.

We need to move before they return fire.

Telisa, of like mind, accelerated away from the *Iridar* toward their target. Magnus felt helpless and exposed as he hurtled out into space with her. Even the lightest ship weapon could vaporize either of them at any moment. Magnus forced himself to let go of the fear. There was nothing to do now but complete the mission as best he could, or die trying.

If I die, I die.

He saw hull breaches in the surface of the roughly donut-shaped Celaran base. It was five times larger than the *Iridar*, but the Cylerans seemed to be winning, at least on the outside. A few spots on the target base glowed. Magnus zoomed in on one such spot and saw a cratered weapons emplacement. He refocused on the nearest hull breach. Telisa had already selected it as a destination.

The sleek forms of Cyleran machines entered the hull breach. The Vovokan spheres cut their own breach into the ship and entered forty meters farther down the hull. Telisa and Magnus were still too far out, but they were closing rapidly.

Magnus wondered if a combat Cyleran was as powerful as a Vovokan battle sphere.

I guess the Vovokan machine would be deadlier, because the Celarans as a whole are so peaceful.

Magnus turned to Telisa, but she charged after them with both suit thrusters. Magnus followed with a more measured pace. He could see gases escaping into space from the breaches.

"The water isn't helping us! Keep bleeding it off!" Telisa said.

"There are robots outside repairing the breaches," Marcant noted.

"That means they've recovered from the remoras," Magnus pointed out.

"I'm not so sure. Those systems should be isolated and designed to work when the ship has taken critical damage," Marcant said. "Of course, we can't be certain since we don't know the Quarus that well."

Magnus arrived at their breach behind Telisa. He jetted inside and landed on a partially melted deck. Blobs of water half the size of a Terran moved within the tunnel ahead, boiling into vapor in the vacuum. He followed Telisa into the alien ship against a storm of water and vapor. He felt the pull of artificial gravity drawing him toward a flat plane on this right. He oriented himself by deciding that direction was "down" and kept moving forward.

He encountered a portal that was somehow retarding the outflow of water into space. Although he had no idea what sort of mechanism could do such a thing, it did not surprise him that the Quarus used such technology. Magnus slammed into the water on the other side of the gateway. Telisa was a dim form swimming rapidly ahead.

The water sloshed violently, coming up to his chest at the peaks. The atmosphere above the liquid was a dense fog. The water pulled Magnus left, then forward. He considered anchoring himself to something, but then he would be sacrificing mobility...

A Cyleran slid up next to him, moving relatively effortlessly in the chaos. It was shaped like a thick, oversized Celaran with three long metal arms instead of three skeletal fingers.

"Can you sense your friends?" it asked.

Magnus saw them on his tactical. He felt a rush of excitement. Could the rescue actually succeed?

"That way," Magnus sent and pointed deeper into the base.

The body of a cyborg next to him started to scintillate. At first, Magnus thought it was some kind of visual communication. Then he realized the Celaran was transforming. Its flat shape rounded into a cylinder as the

Michael McCloskey

arms on one end thickened and lengthened into a three-legged base to support it.

The cylinder turned slightly, then the world flashed. Magnus's suit visor protected his eyes from harm by blocking out part of his view. When it cleared a moment later, the bulkhead was gone. A wall of water poured out beneath a roiling cloud as the liquid boiled away in the low pressure.

"That thing became a... breachmaker," Magnus said on the team channel.

One second it was a flying soldier, the next it had become something else. As Magnus watched, it changed again, taking a torpedo shape so that it could make progress against the water.

"These soldiers are the natural next step in Celaran technology. Super multi-functionality. They can turn themselves into whatever they need," Telisa said. Magnus could not see her in the chaos, but the tactical told him she was within ten meters of his position.

"These bubbles are wreaking havoc with our lasers," she said. "Projectiles aren't much better. There's only about half a meter of water vapor at the top of these rooms."

"Be careful of your weapons," said a Cyleran. "Your friends are coming toward us." The one he had been standing beside had already disappeared into the mist and water ahead.

"We're stuck with what we've got. I left my speargun at home," Magnus told her.

Magnus resolved to catch up to her. The gravity failed just after he pushed off. He splashed through more giant globules of water. He risked one short burst from his exoskeleton to shoot down a corridor and found Telisa covering there from something around a corner.

"We're almost there!"

"Every second counts. They'll be running out of oxygen!" he reminded her.

Telisa and the nearest Cyleran leaped and flew through the water vapor ahead.

Magnus clutched his laser, checked that his breaker claw was still at his belt, and floundered after them in the churning mixture of liquid and gas.

Michael McCloskey

Chapter 17

Caden checked his oxygen monitor. He had only twenty minutes supply left. His suit was dealing with the carbon dioxide problem, but it was not equipped to liberate the oxygen from it.

The team waited in the narrow space above their original arrival chamber. Their weapon lights provided a low level of illumination. Caden could see that the top quarter of the space had been discolored by the grenade, the boil-off, or perhaps the resulting breach repair. Siobhan and Telisa worked to put together a rough contraption to capture oxygen from a simple electrolysis setup. No one was stealthed, as they had decided to contribute their stealth spheres' power to separating more oxygen.

"That attendant got out. Now we have to survive until help can get here," Siobhan said.

Caden supposed she was simply trying to remain positive, but he had to point out his doubts.

"Here? We aren't on the planet anymore, remember?" Caden said.

"Yes, and that's a good thing. The Quarus can live in very deep water, but we haven't been crushed because the interior of this place isn't under high pressure," Telisa9 said.

"The interior is low pressure because it makes the ship safer and stronger. The hull has to contain the pressure against the vacuum outside," Siobhan said.

"Or the Quarus prefer to live close to the surface of the water. Maybe they went deep on the colony planet because they were hiding from us," Telisa9 pointed out.

"I meant we don't know if the others can get here," Caden said.

"They can," Telisa9 said. "They have two ships and most likely, they're on their way."

"We're running out of time," Arakaki said. "Keep working on producing oxygen here. I'll go kill another of these things and bring back the oxygen."

She's so hardcore slickblack.

"You're staring again," Siobhan said to Caden privately.

"What? No. I'm only looking at her. You don't complain when I look at Telisa."

"You were about to suggest you go with her," Siobhan maintained.

"I sorry if this hurts your feelings, but we have to survive somehow," Caden said. "Forget about who's looking at who and get some oxygen. We're going to do the same."

Arakaki dropped off the inner bulkhead and submerged back into the original clear cage area. Caden did not know if Telisa9 had given her approval silently or if Arakaki had left anyway.

"I'm useless here," Caden said on the team channel. "I'm going to back her up."

Telisa9 looked like she was about to say 'no'.

"She has no breaker claw," Caden said, taking out his own claw. "Her laser is going to be screwy underwater, and the projectile weapon—"

Telisa9 nodded. "Go. Come back soon, with or without the oxygen. I'm sure we're about to get at least another half hour's worth."

I think she's being optimistic.

He nodded and slipped into the water smoothly. His mood calmed and he became the machine that had won the Blood Glades.

Arakaki swam through the ragged hole in their clear-walled cage. Caden did a quick 360 check. Dim, cloudy water surrounded them. Caden supposed the earlier drilling and combat had probably polluted the water. He wondered why the ship had not cleaned it by now. Surely the Quarus had life support systems as the Terrans did? Did the aliens prefer their water like this?

It's a good thing. The cloudy water can conceal us now that we're not stealthed.

Arakaki chose a direction and swam on. Caden followed. She slipped past Quarus equipment and found a tall rectangular opening to a curved corridor.

A current pushed at Caden as he joined Arakaki in the passageway.

"It's fighting us," he sent her.

"Would you rather it was sucking us in?" she asked.

Hrm. Definitely not.

"I'm thinking this current is like a conveyor. Makes it easier for them to move around in the ship," she said. "If we're going to hunt them, let's move into the current and meet them head on. I don't want any of them coming up behind us."

"Crazy. We're hunting them, here in *their* ship."

"I have 17 minutes of oxygen left," she said. It was answer enough.

The corridor ended in another opening with vents above and below. The current came from the vents, or at least was encouraged by them. Arakaki held up a fist and knelt down. Caden let himself settle lower toward the floor.

Arakaki grabbed the edge of a vent and pulled herself past its current. Once inside, she stood beside a tall alien machine or container, as if staying out of something's sight. As Caden did the same, he saw her level her laser. She sent him her target sig. He did not take time to examine it, he just passed it to his breaker claw and hid behind a bank of gray equipment opposite her.

Caden looked at the obstruction he hid behind. It might have been a series of shelves, but tubes of various sizes ran up and down through it. Very small tubes with a reddish tint might have been insulation for wires, but he was not sure. Each shelf held bulbous metal objects whose function he could not guess. He peered through a gap between the nearest one at eye level and a support strut of the shelves and saw movement.

One of the aliens worked across the chamber. Its four spider-legs supported the softer, tentacled center body. The long, armored legs made it seem huge, but Caden supposed that the creature might not mass that much more than a Terran. Caden heard a scratching noise come through the water and flinched. At first he thought he or Arakaki had scraped on something and given themselves away.

"We kill it before it finishes whatever it's doing," she transmitted.

The thing stopped working. It shifted its four long spider-legs.

How could it hear that?

Caden saw the legs each ended in a large pincer just like a Terran crab's. He supposed that shape was helpful enough to have evolved on at least two worlds if not a thousand. He glanced upward. On the ceiling above them, he saw a small cigar-shaped machine dart back behind the top shelf.

"They're watching us!" he warned Arakaki.

Arakaki's laser pistol fired. The creature across the chamber recoiled. Its four powerful legs quickly propelled its soft central mass toward the far side of the room. Caden saw it had something in the short tentacles around its body. Whatever the item was, it had an aperture which rose to point at Arakaki.

Caden activated his breaker claw with the alien device as his target.

A wall of force slammed into him. He felt his lungs wrench painfully along with spikes of pain from his eyes and ears.

What the hell?

His eyes hurt. He tried to focus, but all he saw was turbulent water filled with bubbles.

"You busted that thing's power ring, didn't you?" Arakaki said. "All that power vaporized a bunch of water. You're lucky the explosion wasn't bigger or we would have been crushed."

It was just a tiny gun.

"I feel like I *was* crushed," Caden sent. He would not have been able to speak it, as his lungs felt damaged.

Arakaki wasted no time. She swam out and dug into the mass of tentacles with her knife, sending the red fluid swirling into the water.

She stopped. Then large bubbles rose from the corpse. "What's wrong?"

"The pressure wave ruptured its oxygen bladder," Arakaki said. She swam up with her suit's gas intake hose in her hand. She sucked up a few of the largest pockets of oxygen, but many of the smaller bubbles flowed away with the current along the ceiling.

"Quick! Go over to the top of that corridor and suck some of those in!" she urged.

Caden pushed off and swam upward, headed after the bubbles. He got to the top and pulled out his suit's intake hose. He slipped nozzle in place about halfway through the stream, but he sucked up what he could.

"I got half of them," he said.

"We didn't get as much this time. But it's better than nothing," she said. "Back to the others. Maybe they had better luck."

Caden half strode, half swam back through the corridor they had used to get to the room with the Quarus. The water had a red haze to it, the blood of the dead alien they had left behind. Little streams of denser red fluid ran along the current just above the floor.

When they emerged, Siobhan spotted them from a position outside the cage where they had started. She had a clear hemisphere sitting on the flat top of a piece of unknown equipment. The edge of the hemisphere came out over the edge, where wires and a hose entered. From the wires and her suit hose, Caden surmised she had succeeded in separating oxygen from the water.

"How was hunting?" Siobhan asked.

"We brought some back, but not enough," Arakaki said.

"We collected another ten minute's worth. If we make any more, we'll be defenseless. Well, except for an ultrasharp sword."

"Something's wrong," Arakaki said sharply.

There were so many things wrong Caden had no idea which one she might be referring to. She continued before he asked.

"If deadly alien enemies showed up inside your space station, what would you do?"

"Well, if we had weapons, I would defend the ship, even counterattack," Caden said.

"Exactly. We're the fish out of water here... you know what I mean, almost helpless. So why aren't they coming in hard to wipe us out?"

"Maybe this is more of a spy station or a science lab. Maybe there are no troops here," he said.

"Good thinking. But it doesn't feel right, does it? Why are they letting us sit here? We came out to get this one, and what was it doing? I mean, what wasn't it doing? It wasn't waiting for us, it wasn't guarding us. Just working on that piece of equipment."

They had made it to the cage. Suddenly the lights flickered, making Caden wonder how the Quarus prevented shorts in their electrical systems. He supposed they must have had centuries to figure it out.

"Okay... *that's* not encouraging," Caden said.

"No, it's good!" Telisa9 maintained. "It means our friends have arrived!"

I wonder if the Quarus will blow up the whole station to keep from being captured, Caden thought. He decided to keep his doubts to himself.

"Then we need to tell them where we are," Siobhan said.

And we have no attendants left.

"We can either go back to that chamber above the cage and cut our way out again, or we can try and run toward their breaches," Arakaki said.

The room trembled. The water jolted Caden a centimeter or two to his left.

"That direction," Arakaki said, pointing the way he had been pulled.

"We're going to swim *into* a fight?" Siobhan asked.

"They're here to get us," Telisa9 said. "We have to make it as easy as possible. They may be dying for us right now."

That shut everyone up. Arakaki took the lead and Caden followed. They were almost to an exit tunnel when a current pulled them forward. A pocket of gas appeared against the ceiling.

Caden was pulled halfway through the curved tunnel. He collided with Arakaki two times. Both times, their Veer suits protected them from injury, though his rifle reported a partial malfunction after the second hit. They struggled to right themselves.

"Keep going," Telisa9 ordered. "They may self-destruct this base!"

Arakaki reached the end of the corridor a meter ahead of Caden. They swam out into another, straighter corridor. It was wider than the last and had no current. The pressure dropped again. Caden watched water boil away at the top of the corridor. He spotted a machine hanging above them in the middle of the straight corridor. It was next to a hatch as if the machine had dropped out of the ceiling.

"What's that?" he asked.

Suddenly the water around them boiled away even more fiercely. His suit sent his link a warning that the temperature had jumped dangerously.

"It's too hot! Go back!" Caden called urgently.

His suit started to burn his skin. It told his link it had no more heat sink capacity to protect him.

Arakaki struggled to retreat as well. Caden heard himself yell out in pain. They swam back into the curved corridor and met Telisa9 and Siobhan, who pulled them away.

Caden started to recover. He heard Arakaki explain.

"There's some kind of defensive weapon ahead," she said.

"A defense weapon that boils them alive?" Caden asked incredulously. He realized after he said it that he was more rattled than he would like. His comment had no real value to the problem they faced. Arakaki had remained level-headed.

"The water only boiled because of the pressure bleeding off from breaches somewhere," Telisa9 said.

"It might keep Quarus at bay by making it too hot," Telisa9 said. "I don't need to know the explanation. Send two grenades to hit it. Program them for directional detonation, straight into that device."

"I've got one left," Arakaki said, taking hers off her belt.

"I have the other," Caden said. He told the grenade its target was the bulb on the ceiling.

"I don't think this model can swim," Caden said.

"Hold it out of the water and launch it," Arakaki said. She held hers up away from the blobs of water that floated in the room, next to a wall. Caden followed suit.

They unleashed the grenades. The weapons spun away, adhering to the walls above the water. Caden retreated back into the corridor.

Ka-Wump!

Caden felt the impact in his bones. Luckily the shockwave had come through the air, not the water. His link told him the grenade had reported a likely hit microseconds before detonation.

More water boiled off. The current started to pull them again. Caden floundered in the chaotic environment. The walls did not have enough features for him to anchor himself.

"Are we getting pulled out into space?" Siobhan asked. "I'm almost out of air."

"That means hull breaches like ours, only bigger," Arakaki said. "We have to assume it's our friends."

"Find our way to them," Telisa9 said. "Head toward the noise."

In an instant, they became weightless. At first, the mass of water stayed below them. Then large globs of it started to detach every time one of them moved.

"This is crazy. I hope we're winning," Caden said.

"Frackjammers, I hope they know we're on board, too!" Siobhan said.

"They do! That attendant must have told them."

Suddenly a bright flash arced through the room. Caden's external audio sensors fed him a sizzling sound like boiling water.

"What?"

"Electrical arc," Siobhan said. "That was close, but my suit protected me."

A silver torpedo-shaped machine slid around the corner and headed for them.

"Don't shoot! I don't think that's a Destroyer," Telisa9 said.

"Drenched with rain, I've brought oxygen," the torpedo said.

"It talks like a Celaran," Caden pointed out.

I guess it's actually a Celaran cyborg.

"Thank you," Telisa9 said.

173

A section of the cyborg's skin slid away to reveal a row of widely-spaced nozzles. Caden and Siobhan plugged into its body. Telisa9 and Arakaki connected on the other side.

"How is it that our hoses fit this?" Caden wondered aloud.

"I designed the connections for your Veer suit air-vines," The cyborg said.

Caden was impressed. It had designed and altered part of its body to get oxygen to them.

"Thank you so much," Telisa9 repeated. "I've got what I need."

"Grab onto me. I'm supposed to extract you from this dangerous storm."

Suddenly a bar extended from the cyborg, bent in mid-air, grew, and bent back to rejoin the machine's skin. The result was a loop of metal perfect for Caden to grab. A glance told him that a bar had formed for each of the Terrans.

Nice trick.

"This thing can make whatever it needs," he said privately to Siobhan.

"The ultimate in versatility. The Celaran way," Siobhan replied.

"We should capture on of these ugly buggers and study them," Arakaki suggested.

The water lurched to one side, sending everyone with it. Caden avoiding hitting anything, but his already-stimulated adrenal system gave him another boost. Caden's suit told him that another electrical current had surged through the water.

Rumble.

"We're not capturing anything!" Telisa9 told them. "They're mismatching their spinner! Hope The Five get us out of here now!"

"Hang on," the machine said.

The powerful cyborg thrust forward, towing them with it. Caden grunted under the acceleration but held on for dear life. The water pressure rose before him, stretching his body back and pulling hard on his arm. They moved swiftly through the water globules. He was unable to straighten himself out against the resistance but kept his grip. He heard Siobhan curse but saw that she had managed to hook her arm around the bar, keeping her on board.

They took a hard turn in an arc. Caden's legs scraped along a wall, but his Veer suit kept him intact. He caught a glimpse of a Quarus body boiling away into space, forming shards of frozen black blood. Then they sped up again. He saw a melted deck filled with debris spinning about.

Caden emitted an unintelligible sound as the cyborg shot out of a hole with glowing red edges and into the vastness of space.

When it said hang on, it wasn't kidding.

As they left the station behind, Caden looked back and saw at least three breach points in the hull. He watched a Vovokan battle sphere obliterate a Quarus space robot that was trying to repair a breach.

"Secure yourselves," the cyborg said.

What? I'm already—

A ripple passed through Caden, clenching his innards. He felt like Magnus had planted a side kick into his liver again.

Gravity eddies. This is the worst place I've ever visited.

Caden looked ahead. He saw a Terran commando vessel which he assumed was their *Iridar*. He felt a relief beyond what he could remember ever feeling before. An assault bay lay open to receive them. The cyborg hauled them inside and brought them to an adjacent prep room, which sealed off and pressurized.

"Did any of you happen to grab a piece of a Quarus floating around in there?" Maxsym asked them on the team channel.

"If we don't leave now, there will only be pieces of *us* floating around," Marcant said.

"Please don't leave me alone out here," Maxsym urged.

Well, at least he sounds sincere, Caden thought.

"Then why aren't we moving?" asked Magnus.

Caden looked at the ship's navigation data in his PV. The *Iridar* lurched away, spiraling in one direction and then another, barely putting space between it and the Quarus ship.

"The solution is complex," Marcant said. "Adair is doing its best."

Ah. The spinners still have to be matched, so we can barely maneuver.

Caden saw that the Celaran assault ship was also moving sluggishly. The two vessels continued their erratic retreat.

"At some point we'll break away and try to weather it out," Magnus said. "Now would be a good time for crash tubes."

Caden tried to access the layout to find the nearest crash tube. Siobhan grabbed his arm and pulled him.

"This way," she said.

They turned away from each other and went to their own tube on opposite sides of the corridor. For a split second before the hatches slammed shut, they stared across at each other.

"I love you!" she called out.

"I love you, too," he said, but both tubes had already shut. Crash foam blasted in to surround him.

Caden accessed the external sensor views brought them up in his PV.

The base spun wildly. Caden was happy to see that it receded in all the views. He felt sure it was not built to rotate like that. He almost asked if they had been under a spinner's gravity or just force from the spin when the base exploded. The sensors cut back to protect themselves from burnout. A shudder ran through the ship, but they continued to distance themselves.

Already, Caden started thinking standard equipment changes to make and underwater training scenarios to run in VR.

We won't get stuck like that again, he vowed.

Michael McCloskey

Chapter 18

Telisa stared at the four Quarus artifacts that lay before her on an examination table. They were amazing acquisitions, but Telisa could only think about what she did not have: Celara Palnod's Trilisk AI.

"You got all these from the ship? Wow!"

She turned toward the voice and saw Magnus coming into the room. He looked at the items appreciatively.

"You didn't think I could step foot on an alien ship and not pick up anything that wasn't nailed down, did you?"

He shook his head and smiled.

"It's just that we were a bit busy—"

"I know. I was honestly more focused on getting our team back. I only grabbed one of these things on the way out. Thank Siobhan and the other Telisa for pocketing more items while they were trying to free oxygen from that water."

"So what priority is figuring these things out?"

"High. These things are our enemies now," Telisa said slowly.

"But we don't really want to fight them. We only want them to stop attacking the Celarans."

"Yes," she said. They shared a moment of silence. Then she continued, "Whether we try to talk to them again, or have to fight them, either way, the course is the same. We learn everything we can about them. These artifacts will tell us more, so we study them."

"Okay, if you're going to make me, I'll study the insanely cool alien artifacts," Magnus said smiling.

She smiled back.

"When you think of it the right way, our job isn't that bad," she said.

***

Telisa was alone in her quarters. Magnus had invited her to lunch, but she had not yet met him; she had to speak with Lee first. Telisa did not want any of the other team members to be aware of the conversation. It would make them suspect her plans before she was ready to defend them.

She created a channel and added Lee.

The Celaran connected quickly. She added a video feed from a ceiling optical monitor, allowing Telisa to see the Celaran flitting around the wide space of the cafeteria. The alien had added a live vine from outside the temple and started to grow it from one corner of the room.

"Yes?"

Telisa added her own video feed so Lee could see her as well.

"Hi, Lee. I was going through the information you gathered from the Trilisk vine temple and I had a question. There was some kind of Celaran-like creature in one of those columns. Is it another hybrid like the huge flyers that can manufacture their own food from the sunlight?"

"No," Lee said. She halted in midair, drooping slightly.

"What can you tell me about that thing?"

Lee flipped in the air and flew into the corner where the vine grew.

"These creatures were our genetic relatives. They lived like us, drinking sweet sap, but they lived down among the roots. That's why they were so strong and dangerous. They had to be strong and use natural weapons to survive since they could not fly away."

"We haven't seen any of them. Did they only live on Celara Palnod? You didn't bring any to live on the colony planets?"

Lee flipped again and shimmered in agitation.

"They are all dead. Gone long before the Destroyers came."

"So these creatures went extinct... how long ago?" she asked.

"It would be a few hundred Sol years since the last one crawled on the stems," Lee said.

"That's all? What happened?"

Lee stopped again and slowly floated downward. She grasped a rubbery roosting cord with one hand and hung from it loosely.

"They were like the ground things. Predator underleaf. Our races competed from primitive times when there was not enough sap, before we turned the vines into much richer sources of food. We learned to keep them from hurting us. Eventually, they all died."

"Really? You mean you... killed them all?"

Lee flew under a table, then back out and found another corner. Telisa recognized the strange flight patterns as a fearful retreat.

"We do not have that word. They were smart, but we were smarter. We learned to protect ourselves with tools and traps. They had tools, too, but ours advanced faster than theirs, possibly because there were more of us on the vines."

"How did that result in their extinction?"

"We isolated them from us. We only meant to protect ourselves, but eventually, they died off. They could not compete with us, and they were not able to adapt to our ever-increasing restrictions. Knowing what we know today, we would not have done that."

Telisa decided the information was too important to keep to herself, despite her earlier desire to inquire discreetly. She had her link share the conversation log with Maxsym.

"Thank you, Lee. That's very sad, but also very interesting," Telisa said.

Within a minute Maxsym had caught up and joined the conversation.

"Amazing! You shared your home planet with another intelligent species! And one quite similar to your own. The many similarities mean that you must share a large percentage of your genome with the extinct creatures," Maxsym said.

"Given our own beginnings and all the wars Terrans have had, it's not surprising for such a situation to end with the extinction of one of the intelligent species," Telisa said.

"I agree. Interesting though, that the more passive of the species won out!"

Perhaps there was also a starvation event involved that Lee did not mention, Telisa thought. *They may have become very aggressive.*

"Yes, very interesting, but I'm glad the modern Celarans won," Telisa said. She retreated to her quarters to continue to contemplate her plan of action.

***

"We just got the entire team back intact. That alone was a miracle. Now you want to go and commit suicide?" Magnus said. His voice rose, but he stopped short of shouting.

The reunited PIT team lounged in Lee's cafeteria-room, arguing Telisa's announcement that she intended to return to the Trilisk complex. Telisa felt certain that the glowing orb Arakaki reported seeing was Celara Palnod's Trilisk AI.

"The risk is worth it. That thing Arakaki saw is another Trilisk AI, no doubt about it. With that in hand, we would be able to stand up to Shiny and make sure he's dealing with us fairly."

"We'll find another way," Magnus insisted.

"The Trilisks didn't kill our team. That robot or whatever it was teleported them into the Quarus ship," Telisa pointed out.

"And we don't even know why," Caden said.

"It could have been the AI," Telisa pointed out. "Maybe it knew you wanted to fight the Quarus with the cybernetic Celarans."

Stating that theory bought her one second of silence.

"If you go in, any Trilisk inside one of those columns might decide to take your body for a spin," Telisa9 said. "You'll never come back."

"Maybe I do, maybe I don't. If I never come back, it's not your problem."

"Trust me, it's the case where you *do* come back I'm worried about," Maxsym said.

Telisa knew what he meant. If she came back under Trilisk control and tried to do what their Magnus had done...

"Those columns could make a Celaran or Terran host body any time they feel like it," Telisa said. "If there's a Trilisk there that wants out, it's coming out regardless. I'm the leader and this is what I'm doing. Set up more defenses as soon as I leave. Something that will take me out if you sense Trilisk activity. Or run away and go on without me. With the AI, I should be able to take care of myself until I can catch a ride back to... somewhere."

Telisa turned and walked out. She started to work through her link, arranging for a shuttle ride down to the temple site.

Somehow, when she arrived at the shuttle bay, she discovered Magnus had beat her there. He stepped close to her, blocking her way, and gently put his hand on her shoulder.

"You'll be taken by a Trilisk in one of those columns, and you'll never come back," Magnus said.

"If I don't come back you'll all be fine," Telisa argued. "Things will become more normal, with one Telisa and one Magnus and no host bodies to worry about."

"That's ridiculous. You know we wouldn't all just shrug and go on like nothing happened."

"I want to do this. I want to take this risk. If this is the price of being a host body, then I'll pay it. But if I get in there and walk out with the AI, then we've finally taken a real step toward deciding our own fate."

Magnus embraced her, then stepped aside.

"Then bring back the AI," he said.

Telisa nodded. She took a long look at Magnus.

This is worth it.

Telisa climbed into the shuttle alone and closed it up. The Terran shuttle was an armored pod designed to carry a squad of men and machines into battle. It had many droppable decoys and electronic countermeasures to hide its approach. None of that mattered now.

She thought about the AIs as the shuttle left the *Iridar* and headed for the temple site below. How many had the mighty Trilisks ever constructed? They obviously lasted a long time, but the ones they had found were not as powerful as they once must have been. Did they break down? Run out of energy? Go insane from aeons without their builders?

Shiny had at least two of them. One Trilisk AI seemed an amazing boon, yet she wondered if they would be able to use it anywhere near as well as Shiny had learned to do.

Before she knew it, the shuttle was telling her it had settled in on the surface.

Time to go.

Telisa found a bag in the shuttle and brought it with her.

I keep all my Trilisk AIs in this bag, she thought. The ridiculous internal monologue helped to calm her a bit. Going into action did not generally make her nervous any more; but she was a host body, so if there was a Trilisk presence at the complex, she would have no control over her fate. The enslavement would be almost instantaneous.

Once outside, she oriented herself on a link map and set out. She walked toward the mountain of healthy green rising before her. The sickly vines surrounded the area like a reddish-green sea around an island.

Telisa felt an increasing sense of unease as she approached.

What is so wrong here?

She paused to look around and listen with her heightened senses.

Of course. I'm alone.

How long had it been since Telisa had been so utterly alone? She had grown accustomed to alien planets with a lack of link services, but it was more than that. The team operated in groups, whether on real missions or virtual training ones, and she had not trained to work alone in a long time.

She resumed her progress and came to the same entrance the team had used to enter the Trilisk vine temple. The light of the star was blocked by the thick vines, but her enhanced vision served her well enough.

The original Telisa would use her artificial eye here, she thought. It was strange to think about. She was not the being that had made most of the memories of her life.

Telisa retraced the steps of her copy and her team. She saw the thickened vine alcoves and the trail of hardened vine cover spots the others had noted.

That robot must come out here, she thought. *It steps there, in the same places every time.*

The capstone had been replaced. Telisa supposed it could mean almost anything. Perhaps there were Trilisks down there that wanted to stay hidden, or maybe it was the duty of a robot to come by and close it up. For a moment Telisa even imagined that a party of Celarans had come in

185

and discovered the opening, before she dismissed the idea as extremely unlikely. The real treasure of this area to Celarans would be all the healthy sap, and yet none of them were here.

Telisa referred to the link map Arakaki had given to her.

This is it. Trilisk columns ahead. Time to face the downside of being Trilisk Special Forces.

Telisa descended. She came to the fork and went left as the previous team had. She suppressed an urge to run. Though impatient, she wanted to act in a confident, routine manner, as she imagined a Trilisk in a host body might act. It was most likely of no use. Her behavior cues might fool a Terran system, but anything Trilisk would have to see the truth right away. Still, some stubborn part of her clung to the idea.

Everything remained eerily quiet as she marched through the column rooms. All the columns were fully closed now, so she was denied a live view of the ancient ground relative of the Celarans.

She came to the clear-walled complex. It was a maze of transparent walls, ceilings, and floors littered with opaque objects. She looked at the nearest machine through a glass wall. It looked like two black rings joined at three points by silver rods with a slow-spinning disk floating in the interior.

That is something amazing. It might be something I could spend a lifetime trying to understand.

She looked for signs of the battle that had occurred, but everything looked clean and new. For some reason, she had a crazy thought that maybe there had been no fight with a Trilisk robot at all. Maybe it had all been implanted into their minds.

No reason for that to be the case... it's just that the Trilisks are capable of so much, and they're so distant and unpredictable.

Telisa followed her map and took several turns through the glass walls. No three-legged, three-armed robot came to challenge her. There was a soft sound, the hum of a machine or the gentle flow of air that surrounded her. It was constant and reassuring.

Her sharp eyes saw colorful light wavering through several clear walls. She headed in that direction.

The source was a floating sphere that slowly changed colors as it rotated. Thin rods moved into it with quick precision as it moved, while at other random times, the rods slid back out, floating in space around it.

Is that thing even made of regular matter?

"You must be weak. Been here a long time, I suppose," Telisa said to it. The device did not answer. Telisa remembered the Trilisk AIs did not talk; they just *provided.*

The AI had no Vovokan holder. Telisa suspected that meant the AI would serve anyone in range. She did not have the security enhancement of being able to screen the device from the prayers of her enemies.

I haven't even grabbed it yet and I've already thought of complications.

"Whoever made you and used you here is long gone, I think," she said. "I have need of you, now."

She gently grasped the device and placing it into her bag. It felt like a fuzzy ball charged with static. The moving rods could not be felt, only seen.

And now, we leave. Quickly.

Telisa returned, taking the same route she had arrived by. Her footsteps echoed among the clear walls around her. Telisa could see through parts of the floor. She saw at least six more levels below her.

What was this place?

She thought about trying to stay and investigate. It could be intensely interesting, but she had to prioritize: she had a Trilisk AI in a black bag and needed to get it back to her team.

When Telisa looked back up from the view through the floor, her breath froze in her throat. A large blue machine with three arms and three legs stood directly in her way. The shock almost broke her rhythm, but Telisa managed to keep walking smoothly. She headed right for the machine fearlessly.

I can bluff a Trilisk robot. I do it all the time. The thought passed through her mind as if just thinking it could turn it from a lie into the truth. With an AI in a bag, it might.

Only four more steps and she would run into it.

Suddenly the sapphire machine shot forward. It was fast, even by Telisa's host body standards. One of its three flat sides faced her squarely, with a leg placed on either side of her feet. The forwardmost arm touched her head— and Telisa was instantly paralyzed.

Her back arched, clenched by some unknown force. Her head flopped back, then an intense pain exploded in her chest, right below her sternum. She made a gurgling sound.

This is it. I failed. Please stop the pain. Finish it!

A soft blue light grew at the edges of her vision. The pain peaked, then subsided. Something had changed. Telisa felt different, but she could not pinpoint the feeling.

Her head righted and control of her limbs returned. She looked at the robot and saw that something now floated between them. It was a 2cm thick rectangular slab of black material about the size of her hand, smeared in blood.

Did that come from... inside my chest?

The force released her. She regained her balance very quickly, thanks to her unearthly quick reflexes. She stared at the slab and then looked at her torso. Her Veer suit had a horizontal cut in it just under her breasts. She pried the edges apart to take a peek. There was no blood or scar on her skin.

The black slab floated to the floor. The sapphire robot stepped aside to allow her to pass.

She felt a tickle across her chest. She looked down again and felt her suit with her hands. The long cut had disappeared.

Telisa stared at the sapphire machine. It was a duplicate of the dead robot she had seen on Chigran Callnir Four. They had not learned anything from it. She was pretty sure Shiny had that one now, if it had not been destroyed.

We didn't learn anything before, but this one is operational.

Telisa decided not to chance trying to take the robot with her. She already had exactly what she needed. The AI was of incalculable value.

Still, the black slab was a mystery screaming to be solved. She could not resist it. She knelt down and picked it up, then walked on by the robot.

When she reached the entrance of the glass chambers, Telisa closed her eyes and imagined herself holding the AI in the main lounge of the *Iridar*. Then she opened her eyes and found herself sitting in the lounge. The AI floated above her.

"I'm back," she announced to the team.

She realized she may have circumvented their defenses by returning so directly.

Maxsym will wet himself.

"Oh, sorry about this. I should have come back in the shuttle. I'll wait here until you can complete the checkup. I have the AI, so... don't shoot?"

"Welcome back," Magnus said.

Michael McCloskey

Chapter 19

Marcant walked into a meeting room for a team FTF. He noted that Lee was not present and assumed she would arrive soon, though it was usual for the Celaran to arrive very early and very excited.

When Telisa entered, it felt like the beginning of any other team face-to-face. Then he realized it was Telisa9 from her link identifier. The two copies had differentiated their links so everyone could easily tell them apart.

She was not there to discuss the next course of action for the team.

"I've decided to go back to Earth and report to Shiny," Telisa9 announced carefully. "It will be best if I face him. There's a fair chance he will reconstruct a team for me and give me a new mission," she said with confidence that Marcant found suspect.

"Maxsym, thank you for serving with me. Your scientific breakthroughs are amazing. Jamie, thank you for trusting me even after we fought your fellow soldiers in the UED. I wish you both luck."

Telisa9 approached Magnus, hugged him briefly, then turned to leave. She walked away robotically as if in great pain. Marcant watched her retreat.

I wonder what happened there, Marcant thought. *Tension between the Telisa copies?*

"Telisa allowed the other team's Telisa to sleep with Magnus for a while, causing the other Telisa's guilt to build to the point where she realized she had to go back to Earth and negotiate with Shiny to get her own enhanced leader-Magnus back," Adair summarized privately.

"Have you been spying on them!?" Marcant asked.

"Spying? That implies I had to work at finding things out," Adair said. "This was all patently obvious."

"Adair spends entirely too much time worrying about domestic security," Achaius said.

"At least I'm aware of my surroundings," Adair shot back.

"Well I think the team will function best with only one copy of everybody," Marcant stated to his AI friends, breaking up the conversation.

The "real" Telisa—at least the copy Marcant followed—walked into the room.

"Before we start, there's something you all need to know." She took a flat black rectangle of pliant material and dropped it onto a table.

"A Trilisk machine took this out of me," she said. "Magnus and I analyzed it, and we've concluded that it's a bomb. A bomb laced with the Trilisk toxin compound designed by Maxsym."

No one found words quickly. Finally, Caden responded.

"You've been a walking, talking, Trilisk-killing bomb this whole time?"

"Apparently so. We have no idea how it would be triggered, or why it never showed up on any scans. It's obviously not detonated by anything Trilisk or I would have already exploded."

"Maybe it would go off if you were taken over by a Trilisk," Marcant said.

Telisa nodded.

"A solid possibility," she said.

"You, a host body, just came back from a Trilisk complex, and the toxin bomb has been conveniently removed?" Maxsym said, his voice rising. "Then you could be a Trilisk."

"We checked her—" Magnus started.

"And there are ways around that," Maxsym said sharply. He stood. Arakaki drew her weapon and pointed it at Telisa. Magnus drew a pistol from his belt, but he did not raise it.

"Don't panic. Everyone. Be calm and logical," Telisa said. "If I'm a Trilisk, why would I show you this? None of you had any idea it was there, so why would I... wait. *Did* you know about it? Is this a countermeasure I wasn't aware of? If so... that was very inventive! Good job."

"Adair!?" asked Marcant in shock.

"I wish that was my idea," Adair said. "I did not know."

"One of us put that in you?" asked Siobhan.

"No one?" Telisa asked, looking around. She looked very thoughtful. "Maybe it was Cilreth, and the knowledge died with her?"

"I prefer to think it was Shiny," Magnus said.

"So would I, but if it was Shiny, and it's triggered by being taken over, then why didn't our Magnus explode when the Trilisk took him?" Arakaki asked.

"I don't know," Telisa said. "Maybe he didn't have one, or maybe the Trilisk saw through the trap. After all, that robot spotted this in me right away."

"Exactly," said Maxsym. "It's almost impossible to outmatch Trilisks. They're just too far beyond us." His voice was calmer now, but Maxsym was clearly still deeply concerned.

"It *was* Shiny," Caden said out of the blue, with a far away look on his face. Everyone turned to look at him.

"When I was being interrogated at Space Force Command, they said a duplicate of me blew up a bomb and died. The toxin killed some Trilisks," Caden explained. "I just assumed at the time it was some kind of special grenade that he had used in desperation."

"Imanol mentioned a bomb when he described his mission on Earth," Magnus said. "There was a host body duplicate of him on the island no one had warned him about."

Arakaki lowered her weapon. Imanol returned to his seat. Marcant realized he had been very tense himself. He tried to relax.

When no one else continued, Telisa moved on.

"I was going to announce that Maxsym and Jamie have agreed to join this team... unless recent revelations have changed their minds. If you decide to stay on, thank you. With your help, we may be able to use the Trilisk AI to gain independence from Shiny," she said.

"You mean this team's independence or that of Terra?" asked Marcant directly.

"This team for now. In time, with a careful plan, maybe Sol's as well," Telisa said.

"Why isn't Lee here?" Caden asked.

"I haven't told Lee about the AI. Not yet, anyway."

"Ah. Lee might tell the other Celarans, and they might tell the Space Force—" Marcant said.

"And Shiny would eventually hear of it," finished Magnus. "If he hasn't already noticed it through the battle spheres or the attendants."

"The attendants and battle spheres are totally under our control," Marcant assured them.

Telisa nodded. "Vovokan systems are notoriously labyrinthine," she said. "Just when you think you have them locked down, you discover another layer you didn't consider."

"True, but I have the benefit of Cilreth's many discoveries there," Marcant said.

"And an incredibly intelligent friend to help out," Adair said privately.

"That would be me," Achaius said.

"It's not like we don't have any precedent here," Telisa said. "We used to leave new team members in the dark about the AI until we knew we could trust them."

"Some might consider acquiring the artifact stealing from Celara, even though it is a Trilisk item, not a Celaran one," Achaius pointed out privately.

"It has not had the ability to aid the Celarans in centuries, I suspect," Adair said.

"I'm not judging her actions. Just wondering if this is part of her decision not to tell Lee," Achaius said.

"I would say Telisa has done enough to help the Celarans that she's earned the AI anyway," Adair said. "And, using the AI, she could help them more in the future."

"Or the Celarans could learn about it and use it to rebuild Celara Palnod," Achaius said.

Marcant's eyebrows furrowed as he concentrated on filtering out the AI conversation and listen to the main meeting.

"As some of you know, and maybe all of you have heard, we've found an advanced faction of the Celarans with cybernetic bodies like Cynan," Telisa was saying. "The Cylerans we call them. We've managed to make friends with them. Our mission here is complete. So, what next?"

She asked it rhetorically. Marcant could tell she was about to continue.

"I've called the UNSF fleet into action against the Quarus," she announced. "The Cylerans have been planning more than an attack on that space station. They've been studying the Quarus, and they've located several of their worlds, including a major, established one that could even be the enemy homeworld."

"Before any of you ask me if I really want to start a war that will cost many lives, let me say this: we are already at war. The Quarus won't stop. I intend to deal them a major blow, show them that they can't defeat a united Terra and Celara, then return to negotiations one last time."

"Does anyone have any objections? Or does anyone want out?"

Marcant knew he was not about to bail on the team that had brought him this long line of amazing alien technologies to chew on.

When no one answered, Telisa continued.

"You know what? I'm going to stop asking that. You all know you're free to leave the team if that's what's right for you. If we pick up any new team members, we'll all make sure they know that."

"Cynan has decided to 'return to a comfortable vine' as he put it, and rejoin the Cylerans. I wish him the best," Telisa said. "Let's talk separately about what everyone plans to be doing during the trip. Besides our usual training routines, of course."

The meeting broke up. Maxsym looked like he wanted to talk with Telisa first, so Marcant grabbed some pasta and glucosoda as he left the mess and found his way to his personal quarters to think about his research priorities.

He had just settled down to work on Quarus weapons updates when Telisa contacted him.

"Marcant?"

"Hello," Marcant said, trying to sound airy and positive.

"You enjoy the challenges of understanding alien technologies, yes?" Telisa asked.

"Yes. Absolutely."

She has my attention now. Why would she reiterate what she already knows?

Marcant sensed it the same as Adair and Achaius did: she must have something special to ask.

"Don't sign me up for anything," Adair said privately.

"I'll do it all," Achaius said.

"Well I have good news and bad news then," Telisa said. "You can work on understanding the Trilisk AI."

"I think that must be the good news," Achaius said on the open channel.

"Is that Achaius? You're right," Telisa confirmed.

"Yes. What's the bad news?" asked Adair.

"There's something important we don't have. You see, Shiny had figured out how to put his AIs into a kind of... harness. It allowed his thoughts through to the AI, and screened others out. We need a harness like that so that we can use the AI without having the Quarus benefit as much from it as we do."

"You need me to build a device that prevents the thoughts of thinking entities from being perceived by a Trilisk AI," Marcant repeated carefully. His tone said it all: was Telisa being serious?

"That's right. You can see why it's important," Telisa said.

"I hope you have—"

"No. I have no idea how it's done. It's actually pretty amazing that Shiny was able to do that at all. All I have is some link memories of its appearance."

Uh, I'm going to need help on this one.

"He wants my help!" Achaius said.

"He's talking to me," Adair said.

"I guess I... we... have our work cut out for us on this voyage," Marcant said. "I'll start with our Trilisk detection systems. Maybe the same kinds of energy that indicate Trilisk presence are related to... remote thought detection."

"See? You're probably onto something already. I'll let you work, then," Telisa said and closed the channel.

***

The Trilisk AI interested him more than anything else he had studied before, yet it presented a challenge so lofty that it could take a lifetime to overcome.

197

Marcant had no progress to report when the next meeting was announced a day later. Marcant was thankful it was not an FTF. The meeting channel creation was preceded by a message from Telisa explaining that she had told Lee of the existence of the Trilisk AI, though leaving enough out to downplay its true powers.

Marcant half listened to the news while sitting in a comfortable VR interface chair.

Caden has been preparing a new and interesting virtual training regimen," Telisa announced. "Anything you want to add, Caden?"

"We found ourselves in a new environment inside that Quarus ship. Many of our weapons didn't work, at least not well. We should probably work that environment into our training schedule, and give some thought about what kind of weapons work best in liquid environments," Caden said.

"Good thinking," Telisa said.

"We could practice not fighting underwater at all," Magnus said. "We're at a distinct disadvantage there, so let's not do that again."

"Seems shortsighted," said Adair privately.

"He doesn't literally mean we won't practice that. He just means, we should be smart and fight where we have the advantage," Achaius said. Marcant ignored his little peanut gallery.

"That's my choice, of course," Telisa said. "But we'll add these to our training library anyway, just in case. Marcant?"

"I'm working to help us interface with the Trilisk AI," Marcant said vaguely.

"I thought all we had to do was pray," Siobhan said.

Telisa did not jump in, so Marcant was more specific.

"Actually, it's more about who is *not* allowed to interface with it," Marcant said.

"I see," Siobhan said neutrally.

"The Celarans continue to analyze Quarus language and communications," Marcant said. "So I'll also keep studying Quarus technology with a focus on finding weak points."

"How about you, Maxsym?"

"I, too, have plenty of material to occupy even a long voyage," Maxsym said. "I haven't really dug into the Celaran life forms yet, and of course, now we have Quarus samples."

"Please put the priority on the Quarus for now," Telisa said. "Specifically, weaknesses. Also, some psychological analysis on them would be wonderful."

"Psychology? What do you take me for, a witch doctor?" Maxsym asked.

Marcant stifled a snicker. Maxsym continued before anyone could say anything.

"I suppose that assignment is likely easier than what you've assigned Marcant, so I should not complain. I'll start learning about them immediately and have a full report... during the trip."

"Magnus and I are working on grand strategy with the Space Force," Telisa said. "Lee is helping us to digest the information the Cylerans have gathered."

"I'm analyzing our link memories of the Quarus ship to develop tactics we can practice in the VRs," Arakaki said. "I'll see what I can come up with for underwater weapons, too. One thing that comes to mind is a design for water grenades the UED had developed."

"Siobhan?" prompted Telisa.

"I got a real hand attached. It's harder to get going with it than the artificial one was, but I'm making progress. I'm going to attempt to make a factory ship. We have robots and weapons to make. I'm hoping I might even be able to make our own attendants... perhaps with the help of Trilisk technology," Siobhan said.

A hint to the rest of us that she wants to use the Trilisk AI.

"Good. If you have any ideas that prove valuable, feel free to work on them as well, I trust your judgment," Telisa said. "Send me a quick update if you change your top priority task so I can make sure what needs to get done has someone on it."

She left the channel. Marcant dropped as well.

"We're going to war," Marcant said privately to Adair and Achaius. "I guess Telisa can't let the Space Force and the Celarans handle this on their own."

"It seems reckless to assault the Quarus with such a dearth of information," Adair said.

"There's no choice," Achaius said. "They'll keep coming."

"We have all we need now," Marcant said. *"We have a Trilisk AI."*

Chapter 20

The Space Force fleet arrived in grand order exactly on schedule. A light screen of dozens of robotic ships arrived first, spread out, and provided protection for the other ships that arrived a minute later. For the most part, it was the same fleet that had come to the aid of the Celarans at the colony world.

Telisa had an impulse to schedule an FTF with Admiral Sager, but she knew there was no point—the only reason she was used to meeting incarnate was to hide from the government. In this case, she would be talking directly to them, or at least, a part of the remnants of the pre-Shiny power structure.

Admiral Sager's link sent Telisa a message indicating he awaited her convenience to deliver a report. She created a channel for the meeting and added Magnus.

"Admiral Sager. It's good to see the fleet," she said.

The Admiral added a video feed. She could only see him from the shoulders up. His head looked a bit narrow but not unpleasantly so. He had short black hair and a smooth face. Telisa found the man handsome looking, but not enough so to distract her in any meaningful way. She much preferred Magnus's more rugged appearance.

"That planet looks devastated," Sager sent. "Can you imagine if that happened to Earth? For all that's happened, at least we haven't been heavily bombed or poisoned."

"They're in a terrible situation down there, but my main goal is not to rebuild this planet, but to stop this from happening to more planets."

Sager nodded.

"I understand, though you should be aware that we've brought a lot of relief supplies. Especially the Celarans, who have a lot of that sap they produce at the colony."

"Hurry up and dispense them. We'll only be here long enough to plan our attack."

Attack. I can't believe I said that.

"I'll adjust the schedules accordingly."

"I'll be sending a large intelligence pack from the Cylerans," Telisa told him. "It contains the data their scouts have obtained on the target system."

"That will be enormously helpful," Sager said.

Yes. Who wants to charge in without knowing what awaits us? The PIT team has done that far too many times.

"We haven't had a chance to dig into the data. Let's do an FTF in a day or two to discuss what we learn and plan."

"Of course, Team Member."

Team Member. Sigh.

"I don't see many Celaran ships in your formation, Admiral," Magnus said.

"The Celarans remain focused on the defenses of their new world," Sager said. "New ships arrive there from the Core Worlds every few days, but they want to remain in a defensive posture."

"Well I can't say I blame them," Telisa said. "That planet may be more valuable than Celara Palnod now."

"A Vovokan battleship arrived there recently," Sager said. "Shiny communicated to the Admiralty and the Celarans that it was his contribution to their security."

"Just one? Shiny's so stingy," Telisa said.

"He's paranoid. The norm for his species," Magnus pointed out. "It's probably only there to gather data."

Or search for the AI.

"If I may say so, Team Members, I find it quite puzzling how Ambassador Shiny's crack exploration team shows so little love for him."

"We know the real Shiny, I guess," Telisa said. "Is he still popular back home?"

"Earth still absolutely adores him. Even Space Force personnel, who are much less enamored of him than other Terrans, have a high opinion of him."

"Even the Space Force people who have not visited Earth since his takeover?"

"Yes, they like him too, for the most part."

"And how about the frontier?" Magnus asked.

"Out on the frontier, I don't think they know what to make of him. But they like that he stays out of their business, for the most part."

"Is Shiny going to support this operation?" Telisa asked.

Sager shook his head over the feed.

"So far, he's not interested."

"Then we'll do it without him."

**

Telisa connected with the local commander of the Celaran fleet in the Celara Palnod system. Their translation systems were working well and provided a synthetic name for the Celaran: Storix. Telisa started the meeting with Magnus and Sager on the channel.

"Storix, I'm so glad you and your ships have come to join this fleet. However, I expected that there would be many more Celaran ships built by now," Telisa said.

"There are more, but we haven't brought them to the thickest vine we called home. We don't want to go to this distant vine, either," said the Celaran.

Oh, no.

"You aren't afraid that the Quarus will return to the attack?"

"They may. If that happens, we will defend ourselves as we had once done against our ancient enemy who lived among the roots."

That nasty looking Celaran-like relative they saw in the temple.

"The only way to eliminate the threat is the show them it's not in their best interest. That means aggressively

203

fighting back, taking the battle to one of their worlds and showing them our new alliance."

"We do not destroy vines. If a predator waits underleaf, we find another," Storix said.

"I don't propose that we destroy the planets in that system. We should go there, defeat them, and show them it is within our power to kill them all. Then we will deliver our message, which is, make peace or else. Tell them if we have to come back we will destroy their bases and poison their oceans."

"They probably don't think like Terrans. Clearly they don't think like Celarans, or they never would have attacked."

"You're right, they don't think like us. But surely if they're an advanced, reasoning species, they'll see that continuing the war against our alliance will only bring ruin."

"We cannot go to do this, at least not now. This place needs our help," Storix said.

"I'm sorry to hear that. Maybe we can meet again soon if I find out something that might change your mind, or if you complete rescue operations."

"We can suck sap and flash at each other again soon."

The Celaran commander closed the connection.

"That did not go well," Magnus said.

"Definitely not," Sager said, speaking on the channel only now that the talk with Storix was over.

"Telisa?" Magnus prompted.

Telisa had envisioned the Quarus space fleets and wondered about their history with Vovok.

"A very compelling theory has come to mind," she said.

"What is it?" Magnus asked.

"I may have just realized what's going on with the Quarus," Telisa said.

"Tell us your theory, please," Sager said.

"The same thing that was going on with Terra before we came and removed the Trilisks."

"You think the Quarus are under Trilisk control?" asked Sager.

"It's perfect," Magnus interrupted. "The Trilisks don't want the Celarans, because they're not aggressive enough. And Shiny's race was too fragmented and chaotic. But Terrans—and maybe the Quarus, too—were more ordered and hierarchical, more easily controlled and used to build up for interstellar war."

"But Vovokans and Celarans are not the enemies of the Trilisks, right? It must be some other ancient race they fight."

"This is too strong of a theory to ignore. We need to check that system for signs of a Trilisk presence," Telisa said.

Telisa made herself a note to prepare that investigation.

"Admiral Sager," she said. "Have you had a chance to analyze the intelligence that's been gathered on the target and come up with a plan?"

"I have," Sager said hesitantly. Telisa immediately picked up the cue: something was wrong.

"Yes? A problem?"

"You've seen the same thing I have," Sager said hesitantly. "That system has been heavily fortified by an advanced and xenophobic race. I think it must be their home system. The satellite system makes Sol's defense grid look like a scant afterthought. The other admirals are balking at the idea of attacking that system."

The other admirals, but not him. Is that the diplomatic way of saying it?

"Even with Shiny's tech enhancements for fighting Destroyers?"

"That helps, but Shiny himself has committed no battleships to the effort."

"But we have the Celarans on our side," Telisa pointed out.

"Very few of them. They're only here because this is their homeworld. It was the center of their civilization. They don't want to take the war to their enemy."

"The Cylerans do, and they're powerful."

"The Cylerans are super-soldiers by our standards. But they aren't a fleet power. They're individuals. Think of them as Space Force heavy assault robots," Sager said. "Are we really going to be fighting them at point blank range inside of ships and orbital stations?"

Telisa shook her head. "I didn't think we would at first. And we certainly aren't going to land on a planet and attack them in their own oceans."

"But?"

"But now we have suspicions about the Trilisks. If we can find them—"

"Then the Cylerans would be perfect for precision strikes to remove them," Sager finished for her.

"Yes. The Cylerans are so flexible they can operate in the aquatic environs of the Quarus. And armed with Maxsym's toxin, they would have a good chance to succeed."

"We'll have to ask Maxsym if his compound we used in the poison gas would work in water," Magnus said. "And if it can penetrate Quarus host bodies."

"Let's hope it can," Telisa said.

***

Maxsym's link sent him an interrupt, breaking his concentration.

Telisa. She is no doubt wanting an update.

He accepted the channel, including its video feed. He saw Telisa's face in front of a ship's wall on the Terran *Iridar*.

"Maxsym. Our plans to show the Quarus our strength have hit a rough patch. Have you learned anything interesting about them?"

Interesting?

Maxsym erupted into laughter with a touch of the maniacal in it.

"So much! Everything about alien physiology is interesting!"

"Okay. What would I find interesting?"

"I've managed to discover their method of reproduction," Maxsym said enthusiastically.

Oops. Did I just imply she is obsessed with sex?

"Really? Already?"

"Yes. It turns out, if you break a piece off a Quarus, it eventually grows into another whole individual."

"Wow. Is their knowledge... what is that called? Do they have genetic memory?"

"No. Well, unless their brains are actually separate symbiotic organisms with their own genomes! I believe the individual with the brain piece would stay... itself, and the new piece would essentially have an infant mind. Of course, they may have high tech methods of getting around that."

"If you rip an arm off, wouldn't the arm eventually starve?" Telisa asked.

"Ah, yes, it would unless cared for. I suspect in their distant past, they had preferred places to separate that might have made things easier. But at their level of technology, it's quite likely they're very good at taking care of any piece they end up with and growing it to maturity. I should be clear: I'm speculating here, though I do speculate with some authority."

Telisa smiled.

Maxsym sent her a pointer to his main overview of the project, which showed a three-dimensional representation of a Quarus. More information was easily accessed from dozens of attached panes in their PVs.

"Is it one organism? We saw armored legs very different from the soft central bodies, and you just mentioned that thing about their brains..."

"I was only mentioning an unlikely caveat. Sorry to muddy the water. The samples we have indicate this is just one creature going way back into its evolution. Their legs are probably armored because those parts are the most likely to be exposed to harm. Also, the legs can wrap around the soft part of their bodies kind of like the Cingulata would roll themselves up."

"I have no idea what a Cingulata is—"

"Was."

"Was, but I think I follow you. Their legs protect their soft bodies."

"Yes. And the many appendages on their main body serve as manipulatory organs like our hands. They possess a complex nervous system that makes these short limbs very precise, I'm sure."

"Any other major discoveries we should know about?"

"It's all major from a xenobiological perspective. Ah. They have organs that secrete complex chemicals into the water. I can't figure out if it is a kind of venom, or if they communicate with these chemicals—"

"Slow talking, if that's the case," Telisa said. "Oh, could that explain why they talk in large batches of information?"

"I have no idea. The chemicals could also be to begin digestion of meals before ingestion of the matter, or to mark territory, or for sexual attraction or reproduction... I don't know yet."

"That's good progress, considering you have nothing more than a few tissue samples."

Maxsym took her very literally.

"Oh, I have a lot more to work with. We have water samples from their station, attendant logs, data collected by the Celaran assault force scanners—"

"Still, I'm pleased with the results. Keep working on it. Would you be willing to take out an hour for me to do a favor?"

"Yes?"

"I want you to examine Magnus."

"What? Is he sick?"

Telisa paused.

That is not like her.

"My copy told me that Shiny has altered Magnus subtly. She said that not only are the team leaders always host bodies, but that he had been altered to be more subservient."

"Ah, yes. I know what she's talking about, as we discovered that together. I'm sorry I did not bring that up with you myself. I can fix this."

"Really? Please do. I really appreciate it!"

"All the male team members require a shot," he said. Her face froze. "I do not joke. One dose should take care of everything."

"Wow. Okay. I'll send them your way in the next 24 hours."

"Got it."

"Is there anything else you want to talk about?" she asked.

Maxsym's gaze shifted from hers slightly.

"There is another project..."

"Yes? You like to multitask?"

"I hope you would agree with your copy, the Telisa I was working with previously," he said. He gathered his courage.

"We had been working on the biology of Trilisk host bodies," he said.

"Let me guess: she wanted to keep the advantages and lose the vulnerability," Telisa offered.

"Exactly. Even if it costs some of the advantages, if we could alter the host systems—your system—to no longer broadcast itself as a host and instantly accept control from any nearby Trilisk, it would make all of us a little safer."

"By all means, continue. Let me know if you need samples from me. However, please keep the Quarus analysis as the first priority for now."

"I will, I promise. Thank you."

"Don't thank me, Maxsym. Just keep making progress."

Chapter 21

Telisa checked the crew's status in her PV. It was night by the ship's clock, which had been set to slowly synchronize with Celara Palnod's 25 hour day. She believed that Magnus, Marcant, Jamie and Maxsym were asleep. Caden and Siobhan did not appear to be asleep from the network clues she could pick up without violating their privacy, but it would have to do. As things went on the *Iridar*, everything was as quiet as it got.

Telisa continued down the corridor and came to an armored door at the center of the ship. Beyond lay the ship's bridge and command arsenal. Her link opened the door. She padded past the lounges and smooth display surfaces into the arsenal beyond. There, light of several different colors played against the walls. At the back of the small room, in a corner, floated the source of the light: the Trilisk AI.

Telisa sat on a stack of weapons cases and stared at the Trilisk artifact.

I need your help.

For some reason, she had decided to do this directly before the AI, as if her proximity could affect the strength of whatever tenuous connection all living things seemed to have with the ancient device. Some part of her knew she had decided to do this at night and in secret reflected her shame at the measure.

Telisa closed her eyes and started to visualize. She saw the fleet united in purpose to protect the fragments of Celaran civilization. She saw the admirals, the Cylerans, and the Celarans resolved to stand up to the Quarus aggression. There was no bloodthirst, no battle lust, only the understanding that through strength would come safety.

When she opened her eyes, a half hour had passed. She had an urge to ask the AI to forgive her for attempting such an awful manipulation. Her thoughts turned to the race that had created this device before her.

Did these creatures believe themselves gods? Or is this nothing more to them than a handy tool, a convenient, all-purpose solution to everything from opening a can to fixing a gravity drive?

Telisa was halfway back to her quarters—and Magnus—when her link alerted her. It was Admiral Sager.

"Yes, Admiral?"

"Good news. I've managed to get everyone lined up for the assault. I showed them footage of the Quarus in action a few hours ago, and they've all gotten back to me. I guess they saw the aliens as the ruthless killers they are. All the officers are behind you now."

By the Five! So quickly!

"That's excellent news, Admiral. Keep helping the Celarans down below and prepare the assault plans. Tell them the PIT team has a few high-tech solutions in mind that will give us a critical advantage."

That's understating it.

"That's perfect. It will help seal the deal."

The Admiral paused and looked aside to indicate he had a PV interrupt. After a moment, he turned back to the camera.

"The Celarans have indicated a change of heart. I don't know how you did it, but they're ready to join the attack fleet! I can see why Shiny has put so much trust in you, Team Member Relachik."

"I think you'll find the Cylerans equally motivated. Talk to you in ten hours," she said and closed the channel.

If only I deserved that trust.

Telisa returned to her quarters in silence. When her door opened, she saw Magnus stir in the sleep web. He shifted to regard her.

"There you are! Up at all hours... the Trilisk Special Forces never sleep," Magnus said and smiled at her.

When Telisa did not return his smile, his own faded. His eyes narrowed.

"What have you done?" he asked.

"I used the AI to galvanize this alliance to attack the Quarus," Telisa said.

"What? Why?"

Telisa felt a sense of dread. What if he did not understand? Could she stick with the decision on her own? And what if what she had done really was wrong, and she was causing a war to heat up?

"You and I know the Quarus are bloodthirsty now. Maybe it's the Vovokans' fault, maybe it isn't, but the Quarus are going to keep attacking."

"Yes. I heard the speech you gave to them."

"I really believe it."

Magnus's mouth compressed into a thin line, but he said nothing.

"Say it," Telisa urged. "Let me have it. I want to discuss it. It's not too late for me to undo what I've done, if you can convince me I'm wrong."

Do I want him to talk me out of it or validate my actions?

"You're not any better than Shiny," he said. "You're forcing these men and women... and Celarans, to fight even though they chose not to. You're dictating their actions 'for their own good'. That must be exactly what Shiny's doing on Earth."

"Yes. You're right up to a point—but there's a critical difference. Shiny's doing it because it's optimal for him, whereas I don't want this war at all. I just want to go find and understand aliens and their technologies. But we have to save the Celarans first."

"Shouldn't the Celarans want this for themselves?"

"The Cylerans do want it. They're ready to fight, because they've freed themselves from fear. The Celarans are peaceful herbivores that have always used flight to escape, and they're not emotionally equipped to deal with a problem by fighting. It really is best for them to fight now, though. And that's a conclusion backed up by the Cylerans' willingness to fight."

Magnus nodded. "And the Space Force fleet? Not all of those ships are robotic. All the capital ships, the scout ships, and the older cruisers still have personnel aboard. Many of those people will die."

"What's going to happen if we let the Celarans be exterminated? We'll be next, and we'll be alone."

"Shiny might protect us," Magnus said.

"The Quarus and the Celarans are already more advanced. Shiny can try to catch us up, but is Vovokan technology superior? I don't know. We also don't know how many worlds the enemy controls. We have to ally with the Celarans and stand together, now."

Magnus took a deep breath.

"Your method worries me, but I agree. I don't like what you did, but I like that better than the Celarans dying and Terra being in danger of sharing that fate. We should attack together, show them the new alliance, and then give the Quarus one last chance to stop their aggression."

"That's exactly what we're going to do."

THE END of The Celaran Solution (continued in The Celaran Pact)

From the Author

Thanks for reading! As an indie author, I rely on your ratings and reviews to legitimize my work to those who have not read me. Please review this book on Amazon or Goodreads. Thank you.

Made in the USA
Middletown, DE
16 January 2023

22254847R00126